It was the prom dress Robin had dreamed of. . . .

The dress was made of deep scallops of creamy lace. It had long sleeves and a high lace collar. It glowed there in the dark closet as if it were lighted from within.

It was the prom dress Robin had dreamed of, truly a Cinderella dress that could transform even the plainest girl into a princess.

Taking the dress from its padded hanger, she held it against herself. It rustled softly, clinging to her, almost begging her to wear it. It had been in its dark prison too long. A dress like that didn't deserve to be hidden away.

"Miss Catherine . . . it's just exactly what I always dreamed of wearing to the prom. I was wondering if you would let me take it, just this one time. I know it must be very special to you, but I'd be *so* careful."

Miss Catherine rose from her chair and walked to the big window that looked out on the street. "Robin, you don't know what you're asking. . . . No, dear. The dress *must not* leave this house."

Other Point paperbacks you will enjoy:

The Lifeguard
by Richie Tankersley Cusick

Twisted
by R. L. Stine

The Baby-sitter
by R. L. Stine

Slumber Party
by Christopher Pike

Weekend
by Christopher Pike

Through the Hidden Door
by Rosemary Wells

The Tricksters
by Margaret Mahy

Ghost Host
by Marilyn Singer

point

PROM DRESS

Lael Littke

SCHOLASTIC INC.
New York Toronto London Auckland Sydney

ISBN 0-590-44237-6

12 11 10 9 8 7 6 5 4 3 2   0 1 2 3 4 5/9

Printed in the U.S.A.   01

First Scholastic printing, May 1989

*For my brother George,
who shared Dracula with me
in front of the old kitchen stove
on cold winter nights*

Chapter 1

The dress still hung there in the dark attic closet where Rowena had put it on that sodden morning after her sister's accident. It hadn't changed much through the many years that had passed. Under its shroud of old sheets it was still the color of fresh cream, still as lacy and fragile as it had been that soft spring evening when Catherine first put it on and danced off through the twilight with Michael.

Rowena had watched through narrowed eyes from the round attic window.

And after the hideous accident, Rowena had put the dress in the closet where it still hung, waiting.

Robin was breathless when she caught up to Tyler, but whether it was from running or simply from seeing him, she didn't know. He stood still, watching her coming toward him, his lips curving upward in a grin, eyes lasering delight. All for her.

It was hard to believe.

"Hi," he said softly as she stopped by his side, panting. Bending his head, he kissed her lightly.

"Hi, yourself." She was aware that other girls watched, envying her. Wishing they were standing there in her place. "Why the big grin? Is something funny?"

The grin widened. "Just getting my jollies watching you run. An old leg-man like me can't help grinning when he sees drop-dead perfection."

Pleasure flooded through her, and she felt her face flush. But she was careful to keep her tone flippant. "Well, you can blame these drop-dead legs for my being late. They wanted to go on dancing. Today we were rehearsing for the dance concert. Twenties dances. The Charleston — you know, that kind." She didn't want to bore him with details. "Sorry I'm late."

"No sweat." He started walking toward the school parking lot, touching her arm gently to bring her along with him. "Dancing means a lot to you, doesn't it?"

"Do ducks quack?" she said. "Do lions roar? Dancing is what I *do*. I'd rather dance than. . . ." She searched for a strong enough comparison. "Than anything," she finished weakly.

"*Any*thing?" He gave her a big, fake leer.

She laughed. "Come on now, goofball, let's go. I have to get to work."

A group of girls, their arms full of books, passed them going the other way. Without exception, their eyes went to Tyler. A couple of them said hi, but most just looked.

Tyler Atkins was easy to look at — tall

enough so that Robin had to tip her head back to talk to him as they walked along, but not so tall that they looked awkward together. He had dark eyes like hers, and his hair was thick and the same color as the wheat fields around Forest Dale at harvesttime.

Being Tyler's girlfriend was like winning a lottery. Pure luck. So what if it had been her legs that held the winning ticket? You had to have something a little above average to catch the eye of a guy like Tyler. The trick after that was to keep him. It hadn't been too hard, so far. Probably because she was so different from the girls he'd been used to hanging around with: rich, well-dressed girls with their own cars and time on their hands. Girls he'd grown up with.

Robin was new to Forest Dale, new to Carlyle High. New to Tyler.

"Robin. Robin Whitford. Calling Robin. You've faded out, Robin."

Tyler's voice broke through her thoughts. She'd have to watch that. Tyler liked vivacious girls, girls who could keep up a constant line of bright chatter.

"Sorry," she said. "Guess I was thinking about the dance concert. I have to find a Charleston dress somewhere, or else make one, which is a chilling thought. Sewing machines and I are like oil and water. We don't mix."

"So why don't you ask that old soul you work for if she has a dress?" Tyler suggested. "She comes from the right era."

Robin had already thought of asking Miss Catherine if she had any twenties dresses in that big attic of hers. But you had to be careful how you asked Miss Catherine about anything. Sometimes she'd give you everything but her hearing aid, but other times she'd practically frisk you to make sure you weren't stealing the silverware.

"I'll do that," Robin said. "Thanks for the suggestion."

Tyler opened the passenger door of his low-slung little Trans Am, whistling appreciatively as she settled in the seat with a flash of legs.

"Hey," he said when he'd gotten in the other side, "it's too nice a day just to go home. What say we chug up to the lake and watch the fish jump while we get better acquainted? There's a special rate today — two kisses for the price of one."

She pretended to consider it. "Two, you say?"

He nodded solemnly. "Does that mean yes?"

She reached over to take hold of his chin with her thumb and forefinger, turning his head toward her. "Tyler, read my lips. I have to *work*."

His eyes darkened. "Between your dancing and your working, I hardly get to see you. Where do *I* rate on your list of priorities?"

It wasn't her choice that he came third. But how could she explain to Tyler, who thought money was something that flowed from his father's pocket like water from a faucet, that if she didn't spend so much time dancing she'd never get the dance scholarship, which was her only hope of making it to college? Her father was dead. How could she make Tyler understand that she wasn't working for the fun of it? That even the little money she brought in was needed if she and her mother and her sister Gabrielle were to hang onto the big, old house they'd inherited in Forest Dale?

Tyler's sunny grin reappeared. "Don't answer that. I don't want my ego totally trashed." Gunning the engine of the little red Trans Am, he laid a strip of rubber across the parking lot, which told Robin he was more upset than he let on. He'd been an overly cautious driver lately, not only because she didn't like going fast but also because he'd had a couple of tickets for speeding. Another one or two might mean suspension of his license. Robin couldn't imagine Tyler without the freedom his wheels gave him.

To show that he was at least somewhere on her list of priorities, Robin leaned across the console and let her lips graze his cheek.

He gave a gusty sigh. "It's a good thing prom night is coming soon. The dance concert will be over and you won't have to work. I'll be at the top of your list on prom night, right, Robin?"

"Right," she assured him.

There was no way she was going to tell him that if her fairy godmother didn't come through with a prom dress, she wouldn't be going to the dance, which would probably mean she'd lose him. She couldn't stand to think of that. But she knew Tyler Atkins wouldn't hang around very long if she couldn't manage to go to the prom.

Miss Catherine's big, gray house scowled down at the sporty red car as Tyler braked to a stop. It had never seemed like a friendly house to Robin. In the late afternoon light it looked almost secretive, crouching there behind the two tall oak trees. Sometimes Robin had the impression that the house watched her from its one round eye, which was the attic window. Perhaps it was just Miss Catherine who watched, although Robin had never actually seen her do it. But sometimes, like now, she was sure she saw a curtain twitching and a shadow lurking behind the big front window.

"I guess if you must, you must," Tyler said. "But I can't understand why you want to work for Catherine Macfarlane. Sometimes I really wonder if she's knitting with both needles."

Robin was still watching the front window, but the shadow was no longer there. If Miss Catherine had been watching, she was gone now. Why would she watch like that? Maybe because Robin was late. Very likely Miss Catherine had just been anxious about whether or not she was coming. She worried that Robin might not show up someday, although she hadn't missed a day yet.

Robin brought her thoughts back to Tyler's words. "She's always been nice to me," she said. Miss Catherine paid her well, more than she could earn at McDonald's or a movie theater. The work wasn't hard, mainly just being a companion with a little light housekeeping thrown in. Miss Catherine had a housekeeper who came in daily for the heavier work. "Thanks for the ride, Tyler. I've got to go in now. I'm late."

"You'd be even later if I had my way." He reached over to give her another kiss, this one a little more serious than the one on school grounds. " 'Bye, Babe. Think about me."

She got out of the car and he drove away, waving. She wished she had gone with him.

From her own house next door, Robin could hear Gabrielle playing the piano. The piano was to her sister what dancing was to Robin. The only thing Gabrielle liked about the move to Forest Dale was the big grand piano in the old house.

Poor Gabrielle. She hadn't made new friends the way Robin had. Maybe everything was harder when you were fourteen.

But that was Gabrielle's problem, not hers.

Taking a deep breath, Robin climbed the steps to the front porch and knocked at Miss Catherine's door, wondering what her reception would be. If Miss Catherine was really put out about her tardiness, she could be sitting there, furious and coldly silent, but ready to let Robin have it the minute she walked in. Or she might be bogged down in that swamp of self-pity she frequently fell into. Or then again, she could be totally charming. You could never be sure about Miss Catherine.

"Come on in, dear," Miss Catherine sang out in answer to her knock. "I've left the door unlocked."

Robin went in, walking carefully down the three polished steps from the foyer to what Miss Catherine called her "parlor." It was lower than the other rooms on the main floor and must have been planned that way for some special effect. But the sunken room with its dark old furniture gave Robin the feeling of being in a pit. Shadows never quite disappeared from its corners, and it always felt a little chilly, even on warm days.

Miss Catherine was sitting in the blue-striped Morris chair where she spent a lot of her time. A small fire crackled in the fireplace. It didn't give much cheer to the gloomy room, with its heavy gold draperies and dark Oriental rugs.

Miss Catherine was staring at the flames. She gave the impression of having been there for some time, although Robin was sure she'd been at the window just minutes before.

Approaching from the right, Robin could just see Miss Catherine's profile, delicate as a cameo and still showing traces of the beauty she'd once been. She was small and frail-looking, with skin that was still nice, even though it was criss-crossed with fine wrinkles.

She turned her face toward Robin to say plaintively, "I thought you'd forgotten to come today, dear."

And as always, Robin was shocked by the ragged scar that disfigured the left side of Miss Catherine's face, puckering the skin and pulling the eye downward so that it looked like a gaping wound. Even though she'd worked for Miss Catherine for several months now, Robin had never gotten used to that ugly scar.

"I always come, don't I, Miss Catherine?" she said gently. "Now, what would you like to do today? Shall I read some more from *Pride and Prejudice*? Would you like to look through your photo albums?"

When she'd first come to work for Miss Catherine, Robin had been afraid to take out the old albums where Miss Catherine could see how beautiful she'd been before the scar. But instead of depressing her, the old pictures seemed to cheer Miss Catherine up, and now Robin enjoyed going through the albums as much as Miss Catherine did. She liked hearing the stories of when the twin sisters, Catherine and Rowena, were girls, when they went to parties and dances, when all the young men came to call. They came to see Catherine, not Rowena. Miss Catherine never came right out and said that directly, but she'd say, in her delicate way, "Rowena had a terrible birthmark, you see." Or, "I always tried to share my beaux with Rowena."

The pictures in the old album showed the two girls, identical twins, except that one of them, Rowena, had a dark blotch on the left side of her face. It covered her entire cheek from chinline to eye, from ear to nose. Robin could tell how self-conscious she was about it by the way she hardly ever fully faced the camera. In some pictures she held her head at unnatural angles to avoid having the birthmark show.

Miss Catherine didn't want to look at the photos today.

"Tell me about *you*," she said, leaning back into the shadows of the Morris chair. "Is your young man still coming a-courting? The one with the little red roadster?"

Her quaint phrases amused Robin. "Yes, we're still dating. He brought me here today. But that's not why I'm late. I was rehearsing for the dance concert that's coming up next week. Today we were working on the Charleston."

"Ooooh." The word was like a sigh. "Oh, the Charleston. Michael was *so* good at the Charleston." The right side of Miss Catherine's face smiled. "I still have my favorite Charleston gown, you know. It's up in the attic. Would you like to borrow it for your exhibition?"

Robin couldn't believe it. She'd been worrying about how she might ask Miss Catherine if she had any old dresses, and here she was *offering* her favorite!

"Miss Catherine, I'd love to borrow it, if it will fit me. And if you'll trust me with it."

"Of course I'll trust you," Miss Catherine said. "You're welcome to it, dear. You'll have to go up and get it yourself. I don't think I could climb all those stairs to the attic today."

"I'll be glad to go up," Robin said. Suddenly the day had taken on an element of drama, of excitement. She'd often wondered what was up there in the big attic, behind the round eye of a window.

"You'll have to move some trunks and boxes," Miss Catherine said. "There's a small door behind the chimney. You'd scarcely notice it if you didn't know it was there. Open it up and you'll find several dresses hanging inside. The red one was my favorite . . . but take your pick." She paused. "Except for one. You must not take the lace dress. Do you understand?"

The right side of her face smiled again, but her eyes held a strange, warning look.

The attic was full of boxes and dark shapes of furniture and stacks of books. There was a wicker baby carriage there, and two white iron cribs. Everything was festooned with cobwebs and dust, like decorations for a Halloween party. It was a gloomy place, but the light coming through the round attic window kept it from being frightening. Besides, Robin found a switch that lit up two dangling light bulbs.

The narrow closet door was just where Miss Catherine had said it would be, there behind the chimney, draped with a netting of cobwebs. Robin brushed them aside carefully, watching for possible spiders. Then she turned the knob of the little door, wondering how many years it had been since it had last been opened.

It didn't want to open now, resisting her tugs. It took all her strength to make it swing out on its rusty hinges. She hoped it wasn't warped from a leak in the roof, because that would mean the dresses might be damaged.

But the dresses were perfect. There were just two of them there, although from the way Miss Catherine had talked, Robin expected a whole closetful. Each dress was draped in a yellowed sheet. The flame-colored one was in front, and it was easy to see why it had been Miss Catherine's favorite, with its V-necked top, dropped waistline, and all those slithery fringes. The other was a jaunty, black, beaded one that her friend Cynthie would die for. Robin wondered if she dared ask Miss Catherine if she could borrow that one, too.

But where was the forbidden lace dress? It must be very special to Miss Catherine if she didn't want it leaving its hiding place. If it had brought on that eerie warning.

Robin peered into the depths of the closet,

narrow and dark as a grave. The rod on which the dresses were hung was anchored in the slope of the roof, and right at the end hung another shrouded dress. She reached in to bring it forward, undraping it carefully as she did so.

The dress was made of deep scallops of creamy lace. It had long sleeves and a high lace collar. Like the flame-colored dress, it had a dropped waistline, but the two were worlds apart. While the red one blatantly called out for excitement and dancing and the braying of horns, the lace one spoke softly of elegance and muted music and romance. It glowed there in the dark closet as if it were lighted from within.

It was the prom dress Robin had dreamed of, truly a Cinderella dress that could transform even the plainest girl into a princess. And Robin knew she wasn't plain, not with her soft, blonde hair and wide, brown eyes.

Taking the dress from its padded hanger, she held it against herself. It rustled softly, clinging to her, almost begging her to wear it. It had been in its dark prison too long. A dress like that didn't deserve to be hidden away. It needed to be worn by a girl who would be dancing with a handsome boy.

Holding it against her body, Robin walked over to the old, tilting mirror that stood by the round attic window. Dim as it was, her reflection showed her what the dress could do for her. The creamy color made her fair skin look like old ivory and her long, pale hair look even paler. The contrast to her brown eyes was startlingly pleasing.

She had to have this dress for the prom.

But wasn't this surely the lace dress that Miss Catherine said she couldn't take?

As Robin bent to look closer, the dress rustled sweetly, promising a joyful prom night if she would wear it. Surely she could talk Miss Catherine into letting her take it. Why, Miss Catherine could be a real-life fairy godmother, and Robin would be oh, so careful with it.

She smiled at herself in the old mirror. Then, for a moment, her heart thumped with alarm because she thought she saw a dark blotch on the left side of her face. But when she looked closer, she saw that it was just a ripple in the mirror.

She smiled again, knowing that somehow she was going to wear this dress to the prom.

Chapter 2

Miss Catherine's faded blue eyes misted over a little when Robin showed her the two Charleston dresses she brought down from the attic.

"Oh, my," she whispered. "I wish you could see all the memories that those dresses bring back. Rowena and I were young when they were new, and the beaux were coming to call."

Robin thought of young men with slicked-down hair and baggy pants, the way she'd seen in pictures of the twenties. "Which dress was yours, Miss Catherine?"

"Well, dear." Miss Catherine hesitated. "To tell the truth, both dresses were mine. Rowena could Charleston even better than I, but, you see, she had that birthmark on her face. The beaux all came to take *me* dancing." She examined the blue-veined hands that lay in her lap. "Poor Rowena."

"I'm sorry," Robin said quickly. "I didn't mean to make you sad."

Miss Catherine looked up brightly. "You didn't, dear. It's all past and gone. Now, why don't you try on those dresses to see which one you'd like to take?"

Robin already knew, of course, which dress she wanted. The sleeveless black one with the embroidered beads was gorgeous, but it would look better on Cynthie. It was the flame-colored one with the fringes that Robin was going to wear for the dance concert.

But if Miss Catherine was in one of her capricious moods, she might veto whichever one she chose.

So she might as well ask for both at once.

Robin cleared her throat. "Miss Catherine, could I borrow both dresses? My friend Cynthie is in the dance concert, too. She has black hair and looks like a million dollars in black." Robin held up the black dress.

The right side of Miss Catherine's face smiled. "Certainly, dear. I'd love to see both of those dresses go dancing again. Now, try on the fringey one. I want to see it on you."

"Thank you, Miss Catherine." Robin hadn't realized how tense she'd been until she relaxed. She swooped down to plant a light kiss on Miss Catherine's forehead, then carried the dresses to the downstairs bathroom.

The flame-colored dress fit as if it had been made for her. She twirled in front of the dark, old mirror, making the fringes slither and swish around her body. It was perfect. Almost as perfect as the lacy, cream-colored dress that was still up there in the attic closet.

Maybe she should ask Miss Catherine now if she could borrow *that* one for the prom. She'd know how right it would be. And since Miss Catherine was so mellow right now, she might let her take all the dresses.

She put on a bright smile as she went out to show Miss Catherine how she looked. Nimbly climbing the three steps to the foyer, she used that as a stage to do a little demonstration of the Charleston, remembering as she did so that Miss Catherine had said she and Rowena used to present little dramas there.

Miss Catherine clasped her hands together and put them up under her chin as she watched Robin. "Oh my, oh my," she whispered, leaning back into the wing chair. "Oh my, I can almost see Michael there beside you. Your young man will be dazzled, Robin."

"I'm not wearing it on a date, Miss Catherine. It's for a show. The dance concert."

"But surely your young man is coming to see you dance, isn't he?"

"He said he would. But we don't have a date or anything."

Miss Catherine gave her one-sided smile. "He'll surely ask you for one when he sees you in that dress. Isn't it prom season now?"

"Next week." Now was the time to ask. "Miss Catherine. Tyler — my young man — has already asked me to the prom. I saw the lace dress up there in the attic closet. It's just exactly what I always dreamed of wearing to a prom. I was wondering if you would let me take it, just this one time. I know it must be very special to you, but I'd be *so* careful." She said the words all in a rush, scarcely pausing to breathe.

Miss Catherine's smile faded. "No, dear, it's out of the question."

"It would just be for a few hours," Robin begged.

Miss Catherine shifted in her chair. One hand fluttered to her forehead. "Rowena made that dress, you know. I wore it to *my* prom, with Michael."

"Oh, Miss Catherine, wouldn't it be nice if it could go to another prom?" Robin hated the begging note that she could hear in her own voice. But she'd beg, plead, or stand on her head if it would do any good. The dress *wanted* her to wear it. She knew it. She remembered its rustling promises.

Miss Catherine rose from her chair and walked to the big window that looked out on the street. "Robin, you don't know what you're asking. It's not a dress you'd *want* to wear." Her voice was shaky. Agitated.

Robin followed her to the window. "Yes, I would, Miss Catherine. It's the most beautiful dress I ever saw. And it's still absolutely up-to-date. A dress like that never goes out of style."

"Robin." Miss Catherine turned to face her. "Robin, how can I make you understand?" Her voice was high and tense.

She walked slowly back to her chair and sank down into it, shaking her head. "No, dear. That dress *must not* leave this house." She slid down further in the chair, suddenly looking old and crumpled. "Robin, that was the dress I was wearing when this happened." She touched the ugly scar on the left side of her face.

Robin's left hand flew up to touch her own cheek, remembering that brief moment in front of the mirror when she thought her face was blotched. "Oh, I'm sorry, Miss Catherine. I didn't know." What kind of a hideous accident had happened to Miss Catherine on her prom night? Robin didn't dare ask. "I'm sorry," she said again.

"So am I," Miss Catherine said.

Robin, wearing the flame-colored dress and carrying the black one, was still thinking about what Miss Catherine had told her as she ran up the front steps of her own house. She truly was sorry that Miss Catherine had had an accident while she was wearing the lovely lace dress. No wonder she didn't want anyone to wear it again.

But the accident hadn't hurt the dress at all. There were no rips and certainly there were no blood stains. Robin had examined it thoroughly there in the attic by the light from the round window. And Robin definitely wasn't superstitious.

So why *couldn't* she wear the dress? She glanced back at Miss Catherine's house, half expecting the glow of the lovely dress to show through the attic window. She imagined she heard the dress rustling, calling to her.

Miss Catherine was being irrational, which wasn't unusual. Maybe she'd relent later. Miss Catherine wouldn't even have to look at the dress. Robin could take it away and return it through the back door. Surely she couldn't object to that.

Cheered by the thought, Robin ran across the porch and went inside.

Gabrielle was still practicing the piano, her nimble fingers climbing a chromatic scale. Robin couldn't understand how she could sit there hour after endless hour, staring at black spots on a sheet of paper. No wonder she hadn't made any friends in Forest Dale. How many people do you meet on a piano bench?

Robin hung the beaded black dress in the hall closet. Then she stood in the archway that led from the entrance hall to the living room and said, "Hi, Gabby."

Gabrielle finished the scale she was doing, then glanced up. Her eyes widened as Robin, making the red fringes swing, slunk across the room. Posing, she stood in the bay of the piano like a torch singer ready to burn down the house with an incendiary song.

"Wow," Gabrielle breathed. "Wow, Robin, where did you get that dress?" At fourteen she still looked like a little kid, and now her face lit up like a Christmas tree.

The dress was the kind of thing that would excite Gabby. She shopped for clothes in thrift shops that specialized in cleaning out attics of the old houses in Forest Dale. She wouldn't even look at anything that didn't come from the fifties or earlier.

"Isn't it terrific?" Robin said. "Miss Catherine loaned it to me. It's the one she actually used to wear when she went dancing with her beau, Michael."

"Her *beau*. I *love* it." Gabby laughed as she

got up to look closer at the dress. "Are you going to wear it to go dancing with *your* beau? Is it for the prom?"

"It's for the Charleston number in the dance concert. And I've got one for Cynthie, too." Robin ran to the hall closet and brought back the black dress.

Gabrielle pretended to faint onto the sofa, then leaped back up. "Get Cynthie over here. I want to fix you both up with headbands and long ropes of beads and stuff." She ran upstairs to her rat's nest of a room where she stored all the treasures she found in her tours of thrift shops.

Robin called Cynthie, who arrived a few minutes later, breathless and excited.

"I told Mom to hold everything," she said. "She was all ready to stitch herself to a chair so she'd stay there long enough to sew me a costume." She held up the black dress. "Robin, this is elegant!"

Both costumes were even more elegant when Gabby finished adding accessories. She'd found shoes that looked as if they'd come from the twenties for both of them somewhere in her closet.

When she was through decking them out, Gabby stepped back and looked at them wistfully. "Tyler and Adam are going to fall down dead when they see you," she said. "You'll be stand-outs in the dance concert."

"If you think these are great, you should see the one Miss Catherine is letting me wear to the prom." The words were out of Robin's mouth before she realized she'd said them. She hadn't planned on saying anything. She wasn't sure that

Miss Catherine could be talked into letting her take the dress. Why had she gone ahead and made the announcement before knowing for sure?

But the image of the creamy lace dress shimmered in her mind, and again she had that strong feeling that somehow she'd get it.

"If that dress is better than these, I'd love to shop in her closet, too," Cynthie said. "Are there more like it?"

"No," Robin said. "There's only one."

That was the truth. There was only one dress in the whole world like the one in the attic closet.

Gabby was right about Robin and Cynthie being stand-outs in the concert. Only two other girls had managed to find authentic twenties dresses, but they weren't anything like Miss Catherine's.

As she danced, Robin thought what a difference having the absolutely right clothes made. She knew she looked great, and that helped to loosen her muscles as she did the intricate dance steps. If the dance people from the university had come, as Miss Feldstrom said they would, Robin felt sure she would get the scholarship she hoped for.

Tyler came backstage after the dance concert was over. "Keep your fringes on, Robin," he said. "We're going to a party, and I want you to be a knock-out there, too."

The party was at his house and included meeting his parents, which Robin figured was why he wanted her to look good. The only other guests were Adam and Cynthie. Tyler and Adam had obviously planned it all out beforehand as a surprise.

They watched some old silent movies from Tyler's father's collection, then Robin and Cynthie taught the boys some of the Charleston steps they'd learned. There was a discreet maid who brought in food and cold sodas whenever supplies ran low.

"This is a lifestyle to which I would love to become accustomed," Cynthie whispered once while the boys were putting new tapes on Tyler's sound system.

Robin knew what she meant. She'd thought the old Victorian house her mother had inherited was spacious, especially after the crowded apartments they'd lived in for so long. But you could put about three of her house into Tyler's mansion, and still have room to throw a barbecue for a crowd. The furnishings were new and expensive. Everything was color-coordinated, as though an interior decorator had carefully planned it, which was very likely the case.

But this kind of lifestyle demanded the right clothes for *every* occasion. Now Robin was even surer that she *needed* Miss Catherine's lace dress. It would be a disgrace to Tyler and his whole family if she didn't wear something truly elegant to the prom. She'd have to try to explain that to Miss Catherine. Anything Robin could afford to buy would make her look cheap in Tyler's world.

But what if Miss Catherine still wouldn't let her take the dress?

* * *

Robin thought later that the plan must have formed in her mind right at that moment, because she decided not to take the twenties dresses back to Miss Catherine unwrapped the way she'd brought them home. Instead, the next morning she put them inside a thick, dark blue garment bag. To protect them, she told Gabby.

She hung the bag in the hall closet until it was time for her to go to Miss Catherine's. She spent two hours every Saturday at her house as well as the after-school hours.

Tyler called at noon. "I have a surprise," he said.

Robin laughed. "I loved the one last night. Is this one that good?"

"All my surprises are good."

The telephone line hummed as Robin waited for him to tell her what it was.

"Well?" she said finally.

He laughed. "I was considering not telling you yet. But I had a hard enough time keeping last night's party a secret."

"Tyler, that was so much fun."

"I thought so, too. Robin, my folks thought you were gorgeous. My dad says somebody like you deserves the best, so he's sending us to the Royale for dinner before the prom. And he's providing a limousine to take us there."

The Royale! Robin couldn't even gasp. The Royale was the fanciest hotel in the whole area. She and Cynthie had gone there once, just to walk through the lobby and marvel. It was old and stately and reeked of money.

"Oh, Tyler," Robin breathed. "Oh, Tyler."

She was still floating somewhere beyond cloud nine when she went over to Miss Catherine's, carrying the dark garment bag with the two Charleston dresses inside.

Miss Catherine had to hear immediately about the dance concert and how great Robin and Cynthie had looked. She laughed happily when Robin told her about the after-concert party. She clapped her hands when she heard about the coming dinner at the Royale.

"It's all going to be so totally elegant," Robin said, standing by Miss Catherine's chair, still holding the garment bag. "Miss Catherine, I'd really love to wear your lacy prom dress that's up in the attic. I'd *never* find anything here in Forest Dale that would be that perfect." She spoke faster. "It wouldn't bother me that the dress had been involved in an accident."

Miss Catherine's high spirits vanished.

"Robin, it would bother *me*," she said. "You already asked me about that dress before, and I said *NO*. Don't ask me again." Miss Catherine's pale skin was red with anger, making the awful scar look even uglier.

She shifted around in her blue-striped chair. "Bring me a pillow for my back," she ordered. "And for heaven's sake, will you do *something* to get a little heat in this room? Can't you feel how cold it is? What is it you think you're here for?"

Robin put down the garment bag and scurried to find a heating pad and blanket. She even lit the fire in the fireplace.

Still Miss Catherine complained, and Robin

knew she would *never* agree to let her borrow the dress.

Just before she left, Robin took the two Charleston dresses up to the attic. The closet door opened easily this time. Unzipping the garment bag, she took the dresses out and hung them back on the long pole where they'd been for so many years, shrouding them again with the yellowed sheets.

Then, without even letting herself think, she took the lace dress from the closet, pressed it against her cheek for a moment, and slipped it inside the garment bag. It slid in smoothly, as if it wanted to go with Robin. She zipped the bag closed again. Her heart thumped so loudly that it sounded almost like ghostly footsteps, and she glanced guiltily behind her. Of course, there was nothing there except the shadowy shapes of boxes, and the old furniture, and two white cribs.

Trying to be casual, she carried the bag back downstairs, but she felt as if Miss Catherine's faded eyes were boring right through the dark, thick material. She tried to smooth the bag down as it hung over her arm so that it would look as if it were empty.

But Miss Catherine didn't even mention the bag.

"You'll be happy to hear you won't have to work next week, Robin," Miss Catherine told her as she stood in the hallway ready to leave. "I'm going to Cherry Springs for a few days. Maybe I can get warm there in the hot pools."

Robin's heart lifted. If Miss Catherine was

away, she wouldn't have to face her each day carrying her guilty secret. Maybe she could get the housekeeper, Mrs. Sloan, to let her inside the house while she was gone so she could return the dress. She hadn't even thought about how she was going to smuggle it back in.

But things would work out. The main thing was, she had the dress! The most perfect dress in the world. The dress that would make prom night the most perfect night of her life.

"Have a nice time at the Springs," Robin told Miss Catherine. "I'm glad you're taking a little vacation."

"I used to spend a lot of time there," Miss Catherine said dreamily.

"Oh?" Robin said. Was Miss Catherine going to talk about the old days now, just when Robin wanted to escape with the hidden dress? "Did you and Rowena swim there in the hot springs?"

"Rowena was in an institution there," Miss Catherine said calmly. "An institution for the criminally insane." The right side of her face smiled. "Have a nice time at your prom, dear."

Chapter 3

Rowena insane? Robin could hardly believe what Miss Catherine had said. Rowena, the girl who had made the wondrous dress, which Robin carried so carefully in the garment bag? Robin almost ran from Miss Catherine's secretive house.

Rowena had been insane — *criminally* insane. But a person couldn't pass her genes on to a *dress*.

Robin wondered what terrible thing Rowena had done to be judged *criminally* insane.

Don't think about it, Robin, she told herself finally. Don't think about it.

Actually, it wasn't too hard to pull her mind away from Rowena, because she was having a terrible struggle with her conscience. Robin hadn't *planned* on having a guilty conscience. She hadn't often felt guilty, since her mother had taught her from babyhood to respect other people's property. She remembered once when she was very young she'd taken a green lollipop from Mr. Cameron's candy store and had eaten it surreptitiously under her bed at home. Her mother had dragged her back to the store to tell Mr. Cameron about it and apologize. At the time she'd thought mothers had some magical power to tell when their children did something wrong. It was years later that she figured out that the green lollipop had left its mark on her lips and tongue.

So what was there to show now? As she carried the prom dress, still hidden inside the dark garment bag, into her house, she checked her reflection in the hall mirror to see if her guilt was visible.

She wasn't sure what she had expected to see. Maybe the great inflated balloon of her conscience floating above her head with a blazing neon arrow pointing down at her?

But her image stared back at her, clear-eyed and calm. How could she look so innocent? Her face was positively angelic, like Miss Catherine's when you looked at her from the right side.

But after all, she hadn't *stolen* the dress. She'd just borrowed it for a few days.

Without permission, her conscience bellowed. What would her mother do if she knew?

It wasn't going to be any fun wearing the dress if she was going to drag around a chain of guilt, like Marley's Ghost. Maybe she could smuggle it back to Miss Catherine's attic. But then what would she wear to the prom?

"Robin, is that you?" Her mother's voice came from somewhere in the back of the house.

Robin hugged the garment bag close against her body. Inside, the dress rustled. She held the bag closer to silence the dress. "Yes, Mom. I just got home."

"Come in here, will you? I have something to show you."

"I was just going upstairs." Robin hurried over to the stairs and ran up half a dozen steps. "I'll be right back down."

She wasn't ready to show the dress to her mother, who would probably rush right over to thank Miss Catherine. Whatever she decided to do, she had to wait until Miss Catherine left for Cherry Springs.

Robin clattered up the rest of the stairs, clutching the garment bag. Gabrielle wasn't anywhere around, for which she was grateful. Gabby's dark eyes would probe and poke at the closely-held garment bag until she discovered what was in there.

Robin hung the bag in the far reaches of her closet, behind her heavy winter coat and some dark woolen skirts. Then she took a couple of deep breaths and went back downstairs.

Her mother was reading in the little TV room off the kitchen with her feet up. She worked in a bank and was on her feet most of the time. She said weekends were the only time she could reverse gravity and get a little blood to flow to her head.

"Robin," she said, "your prom dress worries are over."

Robin felt her face grow hot. Had Miss Catherine called? Did she know about the "borrowing"? Her tongue tripped over itself as she asked, "What do you mean, Mom?"

Her mother put down her book. "Remember Gracie, my friend at the bank?"

Robin didn't remember, but she nodded.

"Well," her mother went on, "she has a daughter two years older than you. Gracie and I were talking yesterday and I mentioned that you have a terrific date for your prom. She asked if you have a dress and said Josie — that's her daughter — had a pretty one that had been worn only once. She said she'd be pleased if you'd like to borrow it. She brought it by while you were at Miss Catherine's — and here it is!" Mrs. Whitford flung her arm toward the door behind Robin and sang out, "Ta DA!"

Robin turned. Hanging on the open door was a dress. It was pretty enough, with a scoop neck and simple, straight lines. But it was pale pink, a color that made Robin's coloring look washed out.

Her dismay must have shown on her face, because her mother said, "Oh, honey, I hope you don't mind my telling Gracie that you didn't have a prom dress. I've been worrying myself sick, wondering how we could afford to get one for you."

Robin made herself smile. "It's lovely, Mom. It really is. And thank you for worrying." She took the pink dress and held it against herself. "Listen, Mom, Miss Catherine has this gorgeous prom dress that's been in her attic for years."

Robin's mother sat up a little straighter. "And she's going to let you wear it?"

"Yes," Robin said firmly. She thought of the dress upstairs. The way it had felt in her hands

. . . soft, clinging. She remembered the way it had glowed in the attic closet, almost lighting up the room.

"Is it anything like those Charleston dresses she loaned to you?" Mom asked.

"Better." Robin, still holding the pink dress, did a little twirl in the middle of the floor. "Oh, Mom, just wait till you see how gorgeous it is! But you know how Miss Catherine is. She doesn't like a lot of fuss, so don't say anything to her. She might decide not to let me have it."

Robin's mother nodded, smiling. "I hear she can be very capricious sometimes. Well, when are you going to get this gorgeous dress and model it for me?"

"Miss Catherine's leaving for Cherry Springs soon. I'll have it then." Robin phrased her words carefully. She didn't want to add any big outright lies to her list of crimes. Besides, she *might* decide to take it back and just wear the pink dress.

"Mom," she said. "Did you know Miss Catherine's sister used to be in a place in Cherry Springs for the criminally insane?"

Mrs. Whitford's eyes widened. "No, I didn't. But I guess I shouldn't be surprised."

"What do you mean?"

"Well." Robin's mother's forehead furrowed as if she were trying to remember something. "It's just something Gracie said one day. I told her you worked a couple hours each day for Miss Catherine. She said Miss Catherine is a very difficult person to deal with, but that she has a right to be a little odd, considering what happened to her."

Robin waited for her mother to go on.

Her mother hesitated. "Maybe I shouldn't even be repeating this."

"Mom, go on. It's too late to stop now."

Mrs. Whitford fidgeted, flipping the pages of the book she'd been reading. "Gracie says that her grandmother told her it was Rowena who caused that ugly scar on Miss Catherine's face. She threw acid at her."

Rowena did that? Rowena, who had made that lovely dress for Catherine to wear to the prom? She must have done it that very night, the night of the prom, because Miss Catherine said she'd been wearing the dress when she'd had the "accident."

No, no, Rowena couldn't have done that to her sister! But why else would she have been in an institution for the criminally insane?

Robin swallowed. "Why did she do it?" She suddenly felt a chill in the room and she shivered slightly.

Mrs. Whitford shrugged. "Gracie didn't know. Catherine was pretty and popular, and Rowena wasn't. She had a disfiguring birthmark. Gracie's grandmother figured it might have been jealousy."

"Miss Catherine has never mentioned *how* she got the scar," Robin said in a shaky voice. "She just said it happened on the night of her prom."

"I shouldn't have told you," her mother said. "Forget it. Rowena is dead now. Gracie told me that her grandmother said she died in a fire many years ago. Look, why don't you try on the pink dress just in case Miss Catherine changes her mind about the other one?"

Robin was glad to run upstairs to change, to try to think calmly. Did she really want to wear a dress made by a madwoman? A dress that had taken part in such a horrible scene as the acid incident?

She'd have to take it back. She could do it right now, telling Miss Catherine that she'd forgotten to bring back the black dress. That would give her a reason for going back up to the attic.

But the pink dress didn't look right on her. It was too long and hung like an oversize sack, totally shapeless. She couldn't even imagine wearing it with Tyler.

She took it off and laid it on the bed. Walking to her closet, she dug behind her winter coat and brought out the garment bag. She unzipped it, and the cream-colored prom dress glowed against the dark material.

Maybe *it* wouldn't fit, either.

But it did. It whispered sweetly as it slid down her body, and it molded itself to her even before she did up the little satin-covered buttons that marched down its front. She could see even better now the way it brought out the creaminess of her skin, and matched the soft color of her hair. She looked radiant in the mirror, and just having the dress on made her feel confident and sure of her own charms. In this dress, she would truly be a suitable date for Tyler.

A dress was a dress. It no longer had any connection with Rowena or the terrible thing she had done. That was all in the past.

Robin tossed her head provocatively and smiled at herself in the mirror. She ran her hands down the dress, but as she gazed at herself in the mirror tears formed in her eyes.

The next week it seemed as if everything was going right for her. Miss Catherine left on Monday afternoon. That evening Robin showed the prom dress to her mother and Gabrielle. Robin let them think Miss Catherine had given it to her just before she left.

She tried it on for them, and their delight was almost as great as her own.

"Oh." Gabby's little face wore the wistful look that was becoming familiar to Robin. "I wonder if Miss Catherine would let *me* have that dress when *I* go to a prom." She flushed a little. "Of course, I'll never meet anybody like Tyler to take me."

"Sure you will, Gabby," Robin assured her. But she doubted it. There wasn't *anybody* else like Tyler in the whole world, any more than there was another dress like this one. "But I wouldn't say anything to Miss Catherine about it till the time comes."

Gabby's prom was two years away. By then she'd have forgotten about the dress.

On Tuesday Miss Feldstrom kept Robin after dance class to tell her that she'd heard from her friend at the university.

"They're going to offer you the scholarship," she said. "Marge says it's been a long time since she's seen a girl with so much talent."

"Oh," Robin gasped. "Oh!" She grabbed Miss Feldstrom's arm. "You're sure she's talking about *me*?"

Miss Feldstrom put on a look of fake doubt. "Well, maybe I *did* get the names mixed up. But I'm sure she said Robin Whitford." She hugged Robin. "You've made it, Robin, and I must say I don't know anybody who deserves it more."

Robin threw her arms in the air and did a half dozen pirouettes across the gym floor. "This is the best week of my life!" she said.

It got even better. Tyler asked about what color her dress was, saying he had to know right then. She guessed that he was going to order flowers to match. It made the coming night seem even more romantic.

Tyler came early on the evening of the prom, as if he couldn't wait to be with her. He was so early that Robin hadn't even finished dressing. Gabby, who, along with their mother, had been like a lady-in-waiting helping to deck out a queen, ran downstairs, saying she'd talk to him until Robin made her entrance.

Nervously Robin peered in the mirror to see that everything was all right. She couldn't believe the reflection was actually her own. She felt — and looked — like somebody else tonight. Someone she didn't even recognize, as if she'd put on another girl's personality along with the dress. A girl who knew she was beautiful, and therefore had no reason to worry about the impression she was making.

From downstairs Robin could hear the piano. Gabby and Tyler were playing duets. One of the reasons Gabby liked Tyler so much was that he'd sit there and play the bass part from the book of duets she had. He didn't play as well as Gabby, but he was very good.

When Robin was finally ready, her mother went to the top of the stairs and called, "She's ready. Gabby, how about some music to descend the steps by."

When Robin started down, Mrs. Whitford whispered, "Honey, you're absolutely breathtaking." She giggled with excitement, as if she were seventeen, too.

Tyler came from the living room and stood at the bottom of the stairs, waiting. Now she knew why he'd asked to know the color of her dress. He'd rented a cream-colored tux to match. He stood there smiling up at her, his wheat-colored hair touched by a shaft of light that came from a lamp in the hall. He wore a blue carnation in his lapel, and he carried a small florist's box in his right hand.

Gabby played something slow and majestic on the piano. It was like a scene from a romantic movie. Robin took one step down, and then another. She wished this moment could stretch out for years.

"Gosh, Robin," Tyler said as she came to the bottom of the stairs. "I didn't know I was taking Cinderella out tonight."

She laughed softly. "Who else would be good enough to go out with Prince Charming?"

Grinning, he took her hand. "Come, then. Our

pumpkin awaits." Suddenly he held up the little florist's box. "I almost forgot. This is for you."

The box had a see-through top. Inside Robin could see two gardenias surrounded by some unidentified flowers that were the same color as Tyler's blue carnation.

The corsage was perfect for the dress: delicate flowers that smelled like an old-fashioned sachet. Robin knew a lot of girls were hoping for orchids for the prom, but orchids on her dress would have been overkill. Tyler knew how to do things just right.

"I love it," she whispered.

Gabby was watching, her eyes a little glazed. Robin felt sorry for her, doomed to stay home with a piano for company.

"Your duet was nice," she said. "What was it?"

" 'The Poet and Peasant Overture,' " Gabby said softly, looking at Tyler. "Just a little piece of it."

It was obvious that she had a jumbo-size crush on Tyler. But Robin didn't mind. Gabby was just a kid.

" 'Bye, Gab." She kissed her on the cheek and gave her mother a peck, too. Then she and Tyler walked out into the magic night.

The limousine Tyler's father had provided was long and cream-colored, too. Mrs. Whitford and Gabby came running out with a camera to take pictures as they got into it and drove away.

The car was so big that Tyler said they could have had a game of Frisbee while they traveled. Instead, they sipped sparkling white grape juice, which looked almost like champagne, out of long-stemmed glasses and pushed the buttons that turned on a small TV and compact disc player.

First they stopped off at Tyler's house, where Robin felt as if she'd passed some kind of test when Mrs. Atkins kissed her cheek and Mr. Atkins told Tyler that if he'd like to stay home, he, Mr. Atkins, would be delighted to escort this lovely lady to the prom.

Then there was dinner at the Hotel Royale. Something French, with delicate sauces and tiny vegetables.

Heads turned to look at them as they walked into the room, and Robin listened to the soft rustling of the dress.

Even their arrival at the prom, which was at another hotel, was something special. Freddy Finch, the class clown, was out in front interviewing the kids as they arrived, as if it were a Hollywood premiere. He made a big fuss over Robin, saying into his microphone, which was connected to a loudspeaker, that Miss Robin Whitford, dancing queen of the silver screen, had just arrived with everyone's heartthrob, Mr. Tyler Atkins. The kids around them cheered, and people passing by stopped to look.

But the best part was dancing close to Tyler. The band alternated between rock tunes and slow, dreamy ones from the forties, which was appropriate since the evening's theme was "Stairway to the Stars," the theme song of one of the big bands of that era.

During one of the slow tunes, Robin wondered if Miss Catherine could possibly have been as happy with her Michael at her prom as Robin was with Tyler. But that only brought thoughts of Rowena, waiting at home, plotting to destroy Miss Catherine's beauty. Rowena, who was criminally insane.

But what made her think of Miss Catherine and Rowena on this perfect evening? It must have been the dress, the lacy prom dress that rustled with joy, that caressed her body as she danced.

Halfway through the evening the Prom King and Queen were chosen by secret ballot. An actual Stairway to the Stars had been constructed, leading to a platform that held two thrones, where they would sit during the intermission program.

Robin wasn't even surprised when she and Tyler were named king and queen. How could it be any other way on this perfect night?

Hand in hand they climbed the Stairway to the Stars, and almost at the top Tyler paused to kiss her, right there in front of everyone. Robin leaned back lightly against the guard rail that had been built along the stairway. It shook a little, too flimsy to hold her weight. It made her uneasy, and she moved forward quickly, bumping against Tyler. But there must have been a nail sticking out of the rail, because some of the lace on the dress caught and pulled her back again.

She clutched at Tyler. His face filled with sudden alarm as he lost his balance, too. They both fell against the flimsy rail. There was a splintering sound and a gasp from the crowd. The whole

Stairway to the Stars was collapsing.

Tyler threw his arms around her as they plunged downward. Above the dry sound of splintering lumber, Robin could hear the frantic rustling of her dress as she fell down, down, down. She heard someone, or something screaming. Was it her voice? Or was it the dress? The dress! *What if the dress was ruined? How could she explain to Miss Catherine?*

The impact of hitting the floor left Robin dazed. Then the heavy chair which was to have been her throne landed on her legs.

There was a moment of terrible pain, then certainly her own voice screaming.

Then darkness.

Chapter 4

The late shift at Forest Dale Hospital had been
routine, for which Felicia Martin was grateful.
She was tired but not totally exhausted, the way
she was on nights when the hospital had more
emergencies than usual. She had a breakfast date
with Mark for the next morning. If she got to
bed by midnight, she'd be clear-eyed and sparkling by 8:00 a.m., the way Mark liked her.

Mark was a morning person. Very likely he'd
suggest a brisk walk after their breakfast. He
wouldn't complain if Felicia was too tired, but
she liked to please him, because he was always
so caring and considerate.

Mark. Felicia smiled as she plumped old Mr.
Ottley's pillow and smoothed the hospital blanket
over his thin body.

"There," she said, "now maybe you can fall
asleep."

Mr. Ottley was watching her. "That secret
smile's too good for an old bone like me, Felicia.
You must have a fella stashed out there in the
parking lot waiting for you."

"Not tonight, Mr. O, but I'll see him tomorrow."

Mr. Ottley shifted a little, and Felicia knew his hip must be hurting, frozen as it was with arthritis. That wasn't why he was there, but it's what gave him the most pain. His type of cancer was almost without pain, although it was terminal.

But he grinned at her and said, "What's the matter with that young guy of yours? I was always partial to girls with black hair and blue eyes, like you. If only I was 65 years younger, I'd take you dancing right now at that all-night place on the lakeshore."

"And if I hadn't been on my feet all day, I'd go." Felicia turned out the bedside lamp. "Try to get some sleep now." She touched his cheek gently.

Mr. Ottley shifted around on the bed again. "It's not so easy anymore. Even sleep gets away from you when you're my age." He worked up another grin. "Mind if I just lie here and *think* about you and me dancing at the lakeshore? We could do a bit of cheek-to-cheek to a slow tune, and maybe sneak a kiss out by the boat dock."

Felicia was used to being teased by her male patients. She was young and she knew she was pretty, and she had a perfect figure. Even her nurse's uniform couldn't hide that. Not that she wanted to hide it. Or at least she never had until she'd started going out with Mark Hansen.

Actually, she wouldn't mind going dancing at the lakeshore ballroom. But Mark would never take her there. It wasn't the kind of place divinity students went to.

Felicia poked her head inside a couple more doors to say good night to other patients who had a hard time sleeping, then headed for her locker. She was just taking out her purse and sweater when the hospital intercom crackled and said, "Dr. Blake, emergency room, stat. Nurse Martin, emergency room, stat."

Felicia groaned as the commanding voice repeated the message. Stat meant *now*. She pushed her purse and sweater back into the locker, slammed the door, and ran down the corridor. If only she hadn't taken so much time saying good night to all those wakeful patients, she'd have been out of there before the message came on.

But wasn't this what being a nurse was all about? Especially in a small, understaffed hospital like Forest Dale Memorial.

She wondered what was up ahead in the emergency room. At this time of night it could very well be a car accident, and it could be very messy.

A team of paramedics she knew was wheeling in two gurneys when she got there. Dr. Blake hadn't come yet, but Mrs. Turnbow, an older, more experienced nurse, was bending over the girl who lay on one of the gurneys, her long, pale hair spread over the pillow. She was very still under the blanket that covered her.

There was a boy on the other gurney. He was trying to sit up, protesting that he was all right and that they should direct all their attention to Robin.

Robin. A pretty name for the pale girl, who was moaning softly.

Felicia ran to help Mrs. Turnbow with the girl, who suddenly cried out louder.

"She's in shock," Mrs. Turnbow said. "Get another blanket, Felicia."

"Be careful of her legs," the boy on the other gurney yelled. "Her feet are smashed."

Felicia grabbed a blanket and hurried back to the girl. The paramedics were speaking softly to Mrs. Turnbow.

"My dress!" Robin whispered urgently. "My dress!"

Felicia leaned closer so she could hear. "Robin," she said. "Robin, can you hear me?" She covered the girl with the blanket as she spoke.

"Yes." Robin's voice was almost inaudible. "Take care of my dress. Please! My dress! Is it torn? Is there blood on it?"

Dr. Blake arrived. He looked quickly at Robin's legs, then turned to Felicia. "What's she saying?"

"Something about her dress," Felicia told him. "Can you imagine worrying about a dress at a time like this?"

"Get it off her," the doctor instructed. "Cut it if necessary."

Robin's eyes opened. "No! No, don't cut it. I can get it off. You can't cut it." She struggled to sit up but fell back, pale and sweating, her blonde hair covering her face.

"Cut it," the doctor barked. "Get a BP reading."

"NO!" Robin yelled.

It must have taken every bit of strength Robin had to say that.

"I'll get it off," Felicia said.

She began undoing the long row of little buttons. "The dress is fine," she said, bending close so Robin could hear. "Don't worry. I won't cut it. Just relax."

"Thank you," Robin whispered before losing consciousness again.

As Felicia looked at the dress carefully she was no longer surprised that Robin had been concerned about it. It was a beauty, a once-in-a-lifetime kind of dress, elegant and expensive-looking, but old-fashioned and demure with its cream-colored lace. It was the kind of dress a girl kept all her life, just to remind her of a special night.

Prom night, that's what it had to be. It was that time of year. The boy and Robin must have been at a prom. A really special night. What could have happened?

Whatever it was, it hadn't been especially bloody. The lovely dress was undamaged, as far as Felicia could see, except for some lace that was hanging loose.

Felicia laid it over a chair where it would be out of the way. She couldn't help wishing she'd had a dress that lovely for her own prom three years before. She'd been seventeen when she graduated, and a dress like that would have made her prom perfect. But her father liked to make money, not spend it. Maybe that was one reason she'd gotten her own apartment as soon as she graduated from nursing school.

"Miss Martin," Dr. Blake said, "maybe you'd better stay with him." He flicked a thumb at the boy on the other gurney. "Find out how this happened." He motioned for the paramedics to wheel the girl into a cubicle filled with machines that would feed her oxygen and drip life-sustaining fluids into her veins.

The boy was lying down now, pale but alert. "Is she going to be all right?" he asked hoarsely.

"We'll determine what's wrong and begin treatment immediately," Felicia said. She sounded stiff and clinical. But what else could she say? "Would you like to tell me what happened, Mr., uh. . . ." She waited for him to supply his name.

The guy took a deep, quivery breath. "Tyler. My name's Tyler."

She made a notation on the chart she'd picked up. "How did the accident happen, Mr. Tyler?"

"Tyler's my first name. Tyler Atkins."

Atkins. Son of the local multi-millionaire. No wonder the girl had such a gorgeous dress. Anyone an Atkins took out had to be as rich as he was.

Expensive clothes were something Felicia would never have if she married Mark. If he ever asked her. Her father was already worried about her going out with a poor divinity student.

"Since when are you into scrimping?" he'd asked when she'd told him she really liked Mark. "Forget it, Felicia. You can do better than a minister."

But she didn't worship money the way her father did. Sure, it would be nice to have dresses like the one Robin had, but that wasn't what was important.

Tyler Atkins was talking, telling Felicia about the awful moment at the prom when the Stairway to the Stars had collapsed. "We were the king and queen," he said. "We were way up there on the platform, but then everything broke and we were falling. We hit the floor pretty hard, but I've been whapped that hard on the football field. She would have been all right. . . ." He stopped and ran a hand across his mouth. "That's when the throne Robin was supposed to sit on fell right on her feet."

Tyler sat up, looking into Felicia's eyes. "It fell on her *feet*. She's a dancer. Her feet were all smashed, and one foot was sticking out real funny. They'll be able to fix her up, won't they?"

He looked very disoriented. Felicia eased him gently back to a prone position.

"Sure, they will, Tyler." She told him what he wanted to hear. "Now, try to relax. We'll find out how things are going soon."

Robin's mother and sister and Tyler's parents arrived just as Dr. Blake came out. He told them that Robin was going immediately to surgery. He tried to be reassuring, but behind his professional front, Felicia saw real worry.

When she helped Mrs. Turnbow get Robin ready for the operation, she understood why.

Poor little dancer, she thought then. You'll be lucky even to walk again.

Mark was always sensitive to her feelings. "Rough night at the hospital?" he asked when he came to her little apartment to pick her up for breakfast.

"Does it show that much?" Felicia peered anxiously into the mirror by the door, looking at the dark circles under her eyes.

"You look terrific." Mark moved closer and wrapped his arms around her. "It's just that you seem distracted."

Felicia leaned her head against his chest. Mark was perfect minister material, warm and compassionate. The things that really mattered. His broad shoulders looked as if they could carry countless burdens.

"I guess I'm just kind of depressed," she said. "There was a senseless accident last night. A guy named Tyler Atkins and a girl named Robin Whitford." She went on to tell him what she could about the accident.

"I know them both," Mark said. "I don't know Robin well, but I've met her. Her sister takes piano lessons from my aunt Penny. They live on Hartwell Street in the old Victorian house next to Catherine Macfarlane."

Felicia nodded. She'd come to Forest Dale from a little town fifteen miles away, but she'd lived there during her nurse's training, and anyone who'd been around for more than two weeks knew where Catherine Macfarlane lived. She was wealthy and eccentric, a real recluse. People liked to talk about her . . . and her terrible scar.

"I knew Robin came from money," Felicia said, "from the way she was dressed."

"Money?" Mark shook his head. "The Whitfords inherited the house they live in. The father is dead. I think they're just barely getting by. But hey, that's none of my business. What *is* my business is finding some scrambled eggs and toast to bring you up out of the bog."

Felicia grabbed her purse. "Let's go."

She couldn't help thinking that it was no wonder Robin had been so concerned about her dress. She'd probably sunk every penny she had into it. Felicia was glad she'd taken the time to hang it carefully in the closet of Robin's room. It had seemed to light up the narrow closet. In her mind she saw it again, soft-looking and lacy and oh, so desirable. If I could have a dress like that . . . she thought.

She did feel more cheerful after they'd eaten. Mark told funny stories about the things that went on at the divinity school from which he was about to graduate.

"Sometimes," Mark said, "we make bets on what will make the Dean crack a smile. Those who've bet that he will, always lose."

Dean Goudy was a stiff, austere man whom Felicia had seen only once. She'd thought of him as The Great Stone Face.

"None of us are looking forward much to the graduation dinner at his home next week," Mark said, "but it's tradition. The guys say if you want a good job reference from him, you'd better show up."

Felicia was worried about the dinner. The graduates were urged to bring their girlfriends. Rumor had it that this was so Dean Goudy could look the girls over to make sure they'd make good ministerial wives before he gave out his recommendations.

What she was worried about was what to wear. It was to be a dress-up affair, and the only fancy dresses she had were bare backed or off the shoulder or spaghetti-strapped. What she needed was something sweet and demure.

Something like Robin Whitford's dress.

When Felicia went to work on Sunday she found she'd been assigned to care for Robin. The girl was very groggy from the drugs she'd been given for the pain. The operation that had been performed had corrected some of the most urgent problems with her mangled feet, but there would have to be more. The prognosis was guarded as to whether she'd be able to walk again.

Felicia made Robin as comfortable as she could. Then before she left the room, she opened the closet door, just to see if the dress was safely there.

It was. Its demure beauty glowed in the dim closet. It rustled softly as Felicia touched it. It seemed to welcome her touch, clinging to her fingers, inviting her to look at it, to examine it.

She closed the door quickly. She'd have to do some shopping the next week to see if she could find something to wear to the Dean's dinner.

And if she couldn't, what then?

The dress was there. Waiting, shimmering, shining. Almost asking to be worn.

But of course it was out of the question to borrow it, even for one night.

Chapter 5

Robin floated.

There was pain somewhere, but she could drift away from it if she tried. She was suspended in space, warm, soft space, and there was music playing. The sound waves rocked her, and she slept.

The pain found her again when she awoke. It was in her legs. Her first thought was that she must have shin splints from too much dancing. She moved to get more comfortable, and the pain made her gasp.

"Robin," somebody said. "Robin."

"Who's there?" She didn't want to open her eyes. She was afraid of what she'd see. She'd had a dream, such a lovely dream about Tyler and a beautiful dress. They were at the prom, dancing.

But there was more. A nightmare of splintering boards and screams and then the pain.

Something was wrong with her legs.

"Robin," the voice said again. Louder this time.

Robin opened her eyes just a slit. A girl in white stood next to her bed. Only it wasn't *her* bed. It was too high. Too narrow. And it wasn't her room. Where were her posters, her stereo, the bureau on whose top several dancers poised in mid-step? This room was white. Bare. Sterile.

Now she remembered.

"My legs," she said, her voice rising toward a scream.

The girl took her hand.

"My legs hurt." This time the scream descended into a moan.

"I know," the girl said.

A nurse. This was a hospital.

"I can give you something soon," the nurse said. "Something to take away the pain."

Robin moaned again. Her legs hurt. They felt so heavy she couldn't lift them. How could she dance if she couldn't lift her legs?

"I can't move my legs," she said.

The nurse smoothed the hair back from Robin's face. "Your legs are in casts."

"Casts?" Terror made her breathe fast.

The nurse nodded. "The doctor will be here to talk about it in a few minutes. I'll help you get cleaned up now."

Robin moved her head from side to side. She didn't want to talk to the doctor. She wanted to see Tyler. Tyler would come and they'd go dancing again. There would be no casts if Tyler came.

Tyler! Where was he? He'd been there in her splintered nightmare. Her throat was so dry she could hardly say the words. "Nurse, is Tyler all right?"

"Yes," the girl said. "He was here while you were still asleep. He'll be back, and so will your mother and sister." She smoothed the sheet that covered Robin. "My name is Felicia. You can call me that if you like."

Robin licked her lips. There was something else that she needed to know. Something she was afraid to ask of the pretty, dark-haired nurse.

"What about my dress? Is my dress ruined, Felicia?"

Felicia smiled. "It's almost perfect. I looked it over very closely. One seam opened up a couple of inches and a piece of lace tore loose. But there's nothing that can't be repaired. It'll be as good as new after a little needlework."

Robin relaxed as much as she could. She'd be able to fix it before she took it back to Miss Catherine's attic. When was it that Miss Catherine was coming back? She had to get the dress back. She had to, but why? Why was it so important?

"How soon can I go home?" she asked.

Felicia didn't look at her. "As soon as you're well, Robin. The doctor will tell you everything you want to know."

She was being evasive. Robin shifted a little to look at the nurse's face, and the pain overwhelmed her. It was as if something monstrous with iron teeth was chomping down on her feet.

She screamed. The pain, the pain. How could she dance with such pain?

"Hang on, Robin," Felicia said. "After the doctor talks to you, I can give you another shot. It'll be just a few more minutes."

Robin was afraid of what the doctor would say. The pain itself told her more than she wanted to know. She wanted to go home.

But she knew she wouldn't be going home. At least not before Miss Catherine returned from Cherry Springs. How was she going to get the prom dress back to the attic before she came home? Suddenly she wished the dress was back there in the dark attic closet. She wished she'd never taken it, had never even seen it.

"Where is the dress, Felicia?" she asked.

"It's right here in the closet," Felicia said. "Do you want to see it?" She walked toward the closet door.

"No!" Robin didn't want to see it. But she couldn't wish it away, any more than she could wish the casts away. She'd have to deal with it, figure out how to get it back to Miss Catherine's attic. She'd probably even have to tell Miss Catherine.

The thought of facing Miss Catherine, of telling what she'd done, made her shiver. What would Miss Catherine do? What *could* she do? She was small, and she was old. Why was Robin afraid of her? It was irrational, but something about Miss Catherine terrified her now. And Miss Catherine could be irrational, too. She might accuse Robin of all sorts of crimes. She might even call the police, especially if the dress was badly damaged.

Felicia had said the dress was all right, needing only minor repairs.

But what if Felicia was lying to make her feel better?

Robin tried to sit up, and the iron teeth bit down on her feet again.

"My dress," she gasped. "Show it to me now."

Felicia nodded and went to the narrow closet. Taking out the cream-colored lace dress, she brought it over to the bed and held it up.

Even through her pain Robin could see that it was not badly damaged. It hung from the hanger as soft and lovely as ever, shimmering in the light that came through the window. But what was it that made her feel cold again? That frightened her so?

"It's so pretty," she whispered.

Felicia nodded. "It's the most beautiful dress I've ever seen. I can understand why you're so concerned about it."

"Thank you." She couldn't possibly understand, of course, but Robin was grateful for her words.

Before she took the dress back to the closet, Felicia held it against herself and looked in the mirror. "You must have been the prettiest girl at the prom in this. It's just perfect for your coloring. I'll bet everyone looked at you." She smiled at Robin. "I feel sorry for all the other girls who were there."

Robin tried to smile. "I was the queen."

It was funny, looking at Felicia holding the dress. Robin had once thought it must look best on a girl like herself, a girl with light hair and pale skin.

But the dress took on an entirely different aspect near Felicia's dark hair and blue eyes. It still looked innocent and sweet, yet it was —

what? Seductive? Had it looked that way on her?

"You'd look good in it, Felicia," Robin whispered before the pain overwhelmed her again.

Felicia swayed as she held the dress, smiling at her reflection in the mirror.

The doctor came then. He was jovial and jaunty.

"Well, how are we today?" he asked. "I understand the feet are giving us a little pain."

Robin was exhausted from trying to stay ahead of the grip of the awful teeth. All she wanted now was to sleep again, to drift away again to the place where the music played.

"May I have another shot?" she whispered shakily. She felt tears well up in her eyes.

The doctor's manner changed. "Yes." He consulted his watch. "In a few minutes. Is it that bad?"

She nodded.

"Would you like to know what we did for your feet?"

She nodded again.

He talked of bone repairs and steel pins while Robin gritted her teeth and did her best not to scream. She didn't ask him how long before she could walk — or dance — again. If ever.

As he left, he told her that she had some visitors who wanted to see her before she went to sleep again. Robin's mother and Gabrielle came in. Their eyes were anxious, and their faces were tight with worry.

They knew the truth. Robin could see it behind the smiles they tried to present. They knew she wouldn't be dancing again, not with Tyler, not with her dance group, not at the university on her scholarship. They knew her dancing days were over as well as she knew it, even though the doctor hadn't said it.

Tyler knew, too. He came in for five minutes after her mother and Gabrielle went out. She couldn't talk except to ask him if he was all right.

"I'm fine," he said. He stood awkwardly by the bed. "Robin, I wish it were me lying there. I wish I'd been the one to be hurt."

Her throat closed and she couldn't answer. She reached out and touched his hand. He leaned over then and brushed his lips against her cheek.

"I'll come every day," he whispered. "They won't let me stay any longer today, but I'll be back tomorrow." He kissed her cheek again and left.

Robin watched him go. Would he really keep coming? Tyler liked action, not invalids.

After he went out, Gabrielle came back in to say she'd take the prom dress home for safe-keeping.

"No!" Robin said. "Leave it here!"

She wondered why she had said that, since she'd been wishing earlier that the dress wasn't there. But when she thought of Gabrielle taking it, she got that cold feeling again. She didn't want Gabby looking at it, touching it, loving it. And she didn't want little Gabrielle to have to face Miss Catherine's wrath if she found out Robin had stolen her dress. Miss Catherine, who could be so demanding.

And she didn't want her mother to know what she'd done. The disappointment and reproach in her eyes would be more than Robin could stand.

"Okay," Gabrielle said. "I'll tell Miss Catherine when she comes back. I'll tell her you'd like to keep it until you come home."

Robin grasped her hand. "No!" she said. Pain made her foggy. "No, please. Don't mention it to her. She won't mind. She'll be upset after having been at Cherry Springs where Rowena used to be. Gabby, promise me you won't say anything to her."

"What if she asks?" Gabby seemed puzzled.

Robin couldn't think what to do if she asked. But of course she wouldn't ask. She didn't even know the dress was gone.

"Gabby." Robin tried to remember what she'd been going to say, but the pain bit into her legs. "Oh, Gabby," she gasped.

Tears came to Gabrielle's eyes. She patted Robin's hand and called to the nurse.

Robin drifted off, and she floated away from the pain. The music played, and a grand display of bright lights twinkled before her eyes. Or was it the glow from the dress? The light seemed to come from the closet and fill the shadowy hospital room.

Through the light she saw Gabrielle leave.

As if pulled by the light, Felicia went to the bright closet and took out the prom dress again. She held it up against herself as she had done before. She hummed as she checked its length and measured it across her hips.

Then just before she fell asleep again, Robin heard Felicia say, "This would be perfect, absolutely perfect for me."

Chapter 6

Felicia didn't know exactly when it was she decided to borrow Robin's dress. It must have been when Robin asked her to bring it from the closet so she could make sure it was all right. Felicia had held it up against herself so that Robin could see it better. As she'd held it, she'd caught sight of herself in the mirror which hung on the wall over the little shelf where the patients put their get-well cards and familiar knickknacks.

She'd almost gasped when she saw what the creaminess of the dress did for her dark hair and clear, rosy skin. It added warmth to her coloring in a way that the stark whiteness of her nurse's uniform never could, yet with a softness and modesty just right for a minister's wife. It made her feel kind and generous. She could picture herself sitting next to Mark at Dean Goudy's dinner, calm and beautiful in the lacy dress.

At first she thought she'd shop for a similar dress, but after looking closer at it she decided it was one of a kind. Later, after she'd given

Robin the sedative her doctor ordered, Felicia looked again at the glowing dress. She touched the deep lace, then took it from the closet, checking first to make sure Robin was asleep.

Moving over to the mirror, she held the dress up against her body to see if it would fit, humming a romantic tune as she did so.

"This would be perfect, absolutely perfect for me," she said.

But her conscience nipped at her. She *couldn't* take Robin's dress.

Resolutely she took a step back toward the closet.

But the dress clung to her.

She stopped to take another look. It really seemed as if the dress had been created just for her, even though she was built quite differently from Robin, fuller in the bust and wider in the hips.

Suddenly she leaned close to the mirror. What was that odd blotch on her left cheek? Had she smeared something on it?

No, it must have been just a shadow. The cheek was smooth and clear and rosy above the creamy color of the dress.

That's when she knew she had to wear it. No other one would do. Even so, she looked through her closet that night to see if she had anything that would be appropriate for the Dean's dinner. She just couldn't imagine going to the Dean's house in any of her own clothes.

Felicia thought of asking Robin if she could borrow the dress. But it would probably upset her to be reminded girls were going out, going to parties, when she herself was so badly injured. Felicia couldn't ask. The dress would be gone for only a few hours and then would be safely back in the closet long before the time when Robin could be released from the hospital. How could it hurt anyone?

Getting it out wasn't going to be easy. If she got caught, she could lose her job.

Maybe it was too risky. Maybe she should forget the whole thing.

And what if Mark should find out? How would he feel? Ministers' wives didn't take things that didn't belong to them. Of course she wasn't Mark's wife yet, but if Dean Goudy recommended him for a good job she was sure he'd propose.

She couldn't wipe out that possibility by doing something foolish.

Yet she couldn't wear one of her low-cut dresses to Dean Goudy's dinner, either. And it wouldn't be any better to go looking like a frump. Judging from Dean Goudy's own wife, he liked ministers' wives to be stylish as well as pure.

There was a risk either way, whether she took the dress or didn't take it.

The next day Felicia got up early after her late shift and went shopping at the big mall, where she tried on such an array of dresses that it made her head ache. But she found nothing that had both style and that touch of demureness. There was a flouncy lavender dress with long sleeves that was modest and kind of old-fashioned-looking, but when she remembered Robin's dress, that one seemed cheap and tacky.

Still, better to be cheap and tacky than a thief.

Felicia almost bought the dress, but then decided to think about it a little longer. The dinner wasn't until Saturday night.

Then Mr. Ottley died.

His death came near the end of Felicia's Wednesday night shift. It wasn't unexpected. His family was there, alerted by the hospital. There was a middle-aged son from Phoenix, who'd been very successful in something or other and was very proud of the fact. He was also anxious to get back to whatever he did.

Brushing impatiently at the lapels of his expensive suit, he said, "I've got a deal hanging fire in Phoenix. I have to get back. I'm losing money."

He reminded Felicia of her own father, a real estate wheeler-dealer. And of Wally, the guy she'd been going with before she met Mark. Wally aimed to be a millionaire before his thirtieth birthday. His whole focus was on money.

Mr. Ottley's daughter was different. Like her brother, she was middle-aged, but there the resemblance ended. She was a small, pale woman who seemed truly concerned about her father.

"Is he suffering?" she asked Felicia as she sat by his bedside and held his rough, blue-veined hand.

Felicia felt inadequate. What did she know, fresh out of nursing school? She wished she had Mark's caring, compassionate manner and could say something truly comforting.

"I don't think so," she said gently. "He slipped into a coma some time ago. I don't think he feels anything."

There were tears in the woman's eyes. "There were so many things I should have said to him." She leaned over to kiss Mr. Ottley's forehead. "I love you, Daddy," she whispered.

Mr. Ottley died soon afterward. His daughter wept while his son strode about barking orders. He had to get the funeral over with so he could get home to his business. He needed to get in touch with his father's lawyer so they could read the will and get that settled. He could use the money in his new venture.

Felicia tried to maintain the professional calm she'd been trained to show in nursing school, but she felt tears in her own eyes. She hadn't been at this long enough to remain totally detached. Certainly she'd seen patients die before, and she'd prepared bodies to be sent to the morgue. But she'd liked Mr. Ottley and his teasing about going dancing. She wished there could be more dignity about his death, without his son rushing to get him put underground so he could collect his inheritance and leave.

She was so upset that she called Mark when she got home, even though it was after eleven P.M. "Mark," she said, "I need to talk."

Mark didn't even ask what about. "I'll be right over," he said.

He came, and they sat close to one another on her foam-rubber sofa. Felicia told him about the events of the evening and how she felt about Mr. Ottley and his family.

"I should be able to put it out of my mind and go to sleep," she said, close to tears again. "I guess I got too closely attached to Mr. Ottley. I'm unprofessional."

"You're wonderful." Mark shifted so he could put his arm around her shoulders, and she could rest her head against him. "That's what I love about you, Felicia. Your warmth. Your compassion. Your integrity."

Those were the things she loved about *him*. He listened to her as only he could listen, offering sympathy at the right time and being reassuring and supportive when she needed it. He stayed there, warm and comforting, even after she fell asleep still sitting on the sofa. She awoke after two A.M. and told him he'd better go home and get some sleep, since he had to get up shortly after six to go to the part-time job he had at the divinity-school cafeteria.

"Are you sure you're all right now?" His concern showed in his eyes. "I'll stay longer if you want me to."

"I'll be fine," she said.

He gave her a light, sweet kiss and left. The apartment felt empty and cold when he was gone. She loved him so much. She'd do anything to be the kind of wife he needed. She *owed* it to him to look like that kind of wife at Dean Goudy's dinner.

She dreamed that night of wearing Robin's lacy dress and whirling, whirling, whirling across a polished dance floor with Mr. Ottley, who held her tightly and smiled when she gasped out that she had to stop. The dress clung to her body, rustling like the night wind stirring the leaves of trees.

* * *

She took the dress the next night at the end of her shift.

She'd traded her Saturday night shift for a Sunday morning one so she could go to the dinner, and she didn't dare postpone taking the dress until Friday night in case something went wrong.

It was raining the night she took it, and she had worn her raincoat to work. By the time her shift ended, the rain had stopped. She carried her coat with her into Robin's room when she checked her just before leaving.

Robin was asleep.

The room was dark, except for the one light over Robin's bed. The long shadows that filled the room made Felicia uneasy. She almost had the feeling things, strange things, were lurking in those shadows. But when she opened the closet door everything seemed to change. The dress, the beautiful dress, seemed to fill the room with light. Felicia gasped and stood silently looking at every button, every fold in the lace dress.

Felicia took the dress from the closet and draped her raincoat around it. Tiptoeing out into the hall, she looked both ways, then stiffened as the intercom crackled and asked for Dr. Hobart, stat. She stopped, hoping it wouldn't ask for her this time. Where would she hide the coat-covered dress if it did?

But the intercom went silent, and Felicia's racing heart slowed a little. She had to get out of there before anyone stopped her. Holding her breath, she hurried down the brightly lit corridor and out into the night.

Inside its covering, Robin's dress rustled softly.

The look in Mark's eyes when he came to pick her up on Saturday evening made all the risk worthwhile. It was a look made up of love and admiration with just a tinge of something very like relief. Felicia was somewhat amused by the last ingredient, but she understood. He'd seen some of the rather revealing clothes she'd stocked her wardrobe with before she'd ever met him, and very likely he'd been worried that she might have worn one of those dresses for this very important party.

"Wow," he breathed as he stood back and gazed at her. "Wow, Felicia, you're sensational."

She knew how she looked. The dress was every bit as lovely as she'd known it would be, and although it fit a little snugger than it should across her bust and hips, that didn't take away from the air of sweetness that it gave her. She'd bought a pair of cream-colored, high-heeled pumps that showed off her nice legs without drawing attention away from the dress. She'd also bought a little beaded evening bag, in which to carry her lipstick and the money she always took along, no matter where she went.

"Thank you," she said to Mark. "You look pretty nifty yourself."

Nifty was a mild word for the way he looked. Although the party wasn't formal enough to require a tuxedo, it was the next thing to it. Mark had a new, dark suit, which he wore with a white shirt and a dark tie kept from being somber by flecks of red. His short, dark hair was neatly combed back, and his eyes filled with delight as he looked at her.

"You should be the queen of the ball," Mark said softly.

For an uncomfortable second Felicia wished he hadn't said it that way. It made her think of Robin, who *had* been queen of the ball when she'd worn the dress. Then her queenly platform had splintered and her throne had fallen on her. And she now lay on a hospital bed, unable to walk.

But tonight's party was not a ball, and there would be no queen, no platform, no throne. And she'd carefully mended the rips in the seam and the lace where the dress had been damaged by Robin's fall. There was no evidence left of the disaster the dress had been involved in. It was hers for tonight, to love and be loved in.

Felicia gave Mark her best smile as she took his arm and they went out to his car. He gave her another of those soft, sweet kisses as he helped her get settled, and she knew this was going to be a night she'd never forget.

Chapter 7

Dean Goudy's two-story house was impressive, especially with all of its small-paned windows lighted the way they were. Actually, it probably wasn't Dean Goudy's house at all, but merely the home provided for him while he served as the head of the divinity college. There was no reason for Felicia to hope that she and Mark would ever have such a home during his career as a minister.

Not that it mattered. What was a house except boards and nails and paint and carpeting? It was Mark's strong character that Felicia loved, and in that respect he was rich.

Dean and Mrs. Goudy were greeting their guests at the front door.

"Come in, come in," the Dean boomed as Mark and Felicia entered. He shook hands with both of them, then stepped back to get a better look. "Now that's what I call a fine-looking couple."

The Dean was a tall man with iron-gray hair and piercing blue eyes that Felicia was sure could see right through to her guilty secret. Would he still think them a fine-looking couple if he knew she'd really stolen the dress that made her look so fine? But that was nonsense, she'd only borrowed it.

"Thank you, sir," Mark said. He wore a pleased grin as he glanced at her. "Felicia would make anybody who stood next to her look good."

The Dean laughed. "That she would, son. Have you met Mrs. Goudy?" He turned to his wife, who beamed cordially.

"No, I haven't. It's a pleasure, ma'am." Mark's voice was sincere as he gripped Mrs. Goudy's hand, then turned to introduce Felicia.

Mrs. Goudy was as handsome as her husband, tall and gray-haired and regal, but her eyes were gentler. She looked like the kind of person you'd feel comfortable confiding in.

"What a lovely gown, my dear," she said, taking Felicia's hand. "You make it fairly glow."

She knew how to give a true compliment. But Felicia wondered if she imagined a faint air of disapproval as Mrs. Goudy's eyes swept the length of the dress, which felt tighter than it had when Felicia had first put it on.

Surely it was her imagination, because Mrs. Goudy's smile was totally friendly as she said, "Now you two young people go along and visit with the other guests. There are hors d'oeuvres and sparkling grape juice in the library."

She gave Felicia's hand a final little squeeze before releasing it and turning to the next guests.

Several of Mark's classmates greeted them as they walked into the library, a large, pleasant room lined with polished walnut bookshelves. A long library table held several trays of food. Uniformed maids passed around more trays of bite-size canapes.

Everything in sight was elegant and perfect. Felicia was happy, so happy, that she'd borrowed Robin's dress. She would have felt totally out of place wearing the tacky lavender one from the mall.

A young man approached, his eyes admiring Felicia. "Well, hey, Mark," he said, "where have you been hiding this angel?"

Mark laughed. "Watch out, Felicia," he said. "This is Brent, the class Romeo. He forgets every scripture he ever knew at the sight of a pretty face."

Felicia pretended shock. "You mean you have class Romeos even in divinity school? I thought you were all serious-minded and pious here."

Both young men laughed. "We voted Brent the guy most likely to run off with his prettiest parishioner," Mark said. "He's proud of the honor."

Brent grinned. His eyes took in every line of Felicia's figure.

The dress *was* too tight. Felicia wished she'd let it out a little. She could have taken it in again before she hung it back in the closet in Robin's hospital room.

Brent took Felicia's arm. "Come on, angel. Let's find something to snack on before I start nibbling at your ear."

He was just a big, harmless goof-off, and normally Felicia might have been a little flattered by his attentions. Certainly she'd dealt with his kind before, the ones who were attracted by the way she looked and didn't care if she had the personality of a lamppost.

But it seemed out of place here. In bad taste. Through the double doors of the library, she could see Dean Goudy watching them during a lull in the arrival of guests.

She started to pull away from Brent, then Mark intercepted. Smoothly shifting her arm from Brent's hand to his own, he said, "Sorry, Brent, old buddy. Find your own girl."

Brent was amiable about it. "Worth a try." He grinned, and Felicia could feel him watching her as she and Mark headed for the hors d'oeuvres. The dress seemed to tighten across her hips. She took smaller steps so it wouldn't be so obvious, but she could feel the dress ride up just a little in the back.

Mark didn't seem to notice. If he felt anything but proud of her as he introduced her to his other classmates and their girlfriends, he didn't show it.

The other young men had better manners than Brent, even though they, too, looked at Felicia with what seemed like appreciation. Some of the girls were not so cordial, she thought. She was sure they were eyeing her up and down, and then turning to say something to someone nearby.

The dress grew tighter.

Felicia was relieved when it was time for dinner. At least she could sit down then and part of her would be out of sight. She'd have to be careful not to eat a lot, which would only make the dress tighter.

There were two long tables set up in the spacious dining room, with a couple of smaller tables in an adjoining room, which Felicia decided was a family room since it had a TV. There were name cards at each place, hand printed in flowing calligraphy. Felicia looked at the cards in the family room, hoping that was where she and Mark would be, out of sight of the Dean's probing eyes. But Mark led her into the dining room, indicating the places just two chairs down from Dean and Mrs. Goudy.

"Teacher's pets in here," he whispered in her ear, grinning.

So Mark was among the favored few, the ones the Dean would give the most glowing recommendations. *If* he — and she, too — passed this unofficial test tonight.

There was a scraping of chairs against the polished hardwood floors as everyone got settled at the tables. Dean Goudy gave a few opening remarks, saying how proud he was of this year's graduates, a truly outstanding group, under whose direction good work would be carried forth into the future.

Then he said grace, and the maids removed the covers from platters and dishes of food and served the guests.

Delicious odors rose up to tempt Felicia. She'd been too nervous to eat much during the day, and now she was famished. She forgot her resolve not to eat a lot and loaded up her plate with roast beef, scalloped potatoes, and green beans. The room was quiet except for the click of serving utensils against china.

"Enjoy yourselves," Dean Goudy boomed as

he scooped food onto his own plate. "Remember, 'he that is of a merry heart hath a continual feast.' "

"Proverbs: 15th chapter, 15th verse," Mark said, and the Dean led the laughter that followed.

Chatter broke out, and the girl across the table smiled at Felicia. "I've been trying to figure out where I've seen you before," she said. "Where do you work?"

The abruptness of the question startled Felicia, and she flushed a little. Was this someone she should know?

The man who sat beside the girl smiled, too. "Let's replay that one," he said. "I'm Ralph Trimble and this is Linda Worley."

Dean Goudy was watching, and Felicia wondered what he was thinking. Felicia felt sorry for all of them. It was nerve-wracking to be under such scrutiny. In an effort to make conversation, Felicia said, "I work at Forest Dale Memorial Hospital. I'm a nurse."

Linda looked at her. "I knew I'd seen you. You're Robin Whitford's nurse, aren't you? I was there with my sister to visit her a couple nights ago."

Felicia felt her whole body stiffen. Had Linda recognized the dress as well as her? Was she going to mention it, right there in front of Dean and Mrs. Goudy and all the others?

The dress seemed to shrink more, almost choking off Felicia's breath.

"Yes, I'm Robin's nurse." Her voice came out a whisper.

The girl smiled again, more at ease now. "I

knew I'd seen you somewhere, but you look so different in your nurse's uniform than you do in that beautiful dress."

Was she going to say it *now*? Was she going to tell everybody that the beautiful dress belonged to the girl who lay injured in the hospital? That it wasn't Felicia's at all, and never had been?

But Linda turned to Ralph and said, "Robin is the girl I told you about who was chosen Prom Queen and was hurt when the platform she was on collapsed."

Surely if she'd been at the prom she must recognize the dress. How could anybody forget it?

Ralph nodded. "I remember you telling me about it. Didn't you say your sister was there and saw it all?"

The dress was so tight that Felicia was beginning to sweat.

Linda was saying, "Yes, Joanna was there. She's in Robin's class. She said it was all the more sad because Robin looked so beautiful that night in her prom dress."

Felicia realized what she was saying. Linda hadn't been at the prom herself. She hadn't seen the dress. And it was unlikely that she'd have looked in Robin's closet at the hospital. Felicia was so relieved that she took a big bite of meat. She was safe!

"That poor girl," Mark said. "Is there anything we can do for her?"

His kind eyes questioned Felicia. She tried to remember if she'd told him anything about

Robin's dress. Probably not, since she'd been so concerned this past week about Mr. Ottley.

Was that the real reason? Or was it because she'd been thinking right from the first moment she'd seen it that she'd like to have Robin's dress, and the less said to Mark about her the better?

"Nursing is such a caring profession," Mrs. Goudy said. "I admire your choice of careers, Felicia."

"Yes, yes, indeed." Dean Goudy nodded briskly, making his head of iron-gray hair gleam in the candlelight. "Medicine and the ministry, caring for the body and the soul. A fine combination." He smiled at Mark and Felicia.

"*I* think so, sir." Mark turned to smile into Felicia's eyes and she knew this would be the night he'd propose, now that he had the Dean's affirmation.

The Dean went on speaking. "Both professions demand integrity of the highest order. I cannot tolerate the thought that anyone going into either field would lack that quality."

Was he looking straight into her guilty soul? Was he seeing what she was really made of?

Felicia pretended to choke on the meat she was chewing. She had to get away from the Dean's blue gaze.

"Excuse me," she said between coughs. She rose from her chair and started from the room.

Mrs. Goudy rose, too. "Are you all right, dear?"

"I'll be all right," Felicia gasped out. "Something just went down the wrong way. And I think I've spilled something on my dress." She dabbed at her front with the napkin she still held. "I'd better go clean it off."

Everybody was looking at her now. They had to see how the dress was squeezing the very life out of her. She gasped for breath. The seams must be about to split. She couldn't just stand there and let it break apart and fall away from her, leaving her practically naked in front of the entire crowd.

Mark was at her side, thumping her back. "Let me help, sweetheart," he said. "Do you want to go home?"

Yes. She would like to go home. Not home, really. She wanted to go to the hospital and return the dress. She wanted it back in Robin's closet where it belonged.

But how could she explain that to Mark? And how would it look if he left the party now?

"No," she said. "I'll be all right." She coughed some more but not so hard, to show that she was recovering.

"Come with me," Mrs. Goudy said, touching her arm. "I'll give you something to ease your throat, and we'll clean off your dress."

Upstairs, Mrs. Goudy led her to a large, white-tiled bathroom where she took a clean washcloth and wet it slightly.

"Now," she said, "let's see to the dress."

Felicia brushed at the non-existent spill. "It seems to have dried out. Maybe it was only water."

Mrs. Goudy peered at the dress. "I think it's going to be all right, dear. It would be a shame to ruin such a lovely gown."

Wasn't she going to comment on how tight the dress was? How Felicia was hardly able to breathe in it? Couldn't she see how uncomfortable Felicia was? Maybe she'd offer to lend her something to finish the evening in. They could say the spill made Felicia's dress unwearable.

But Mrs. Goudy was taking a small box of cherry-flavored cough drops from the medicine cabinet over the washbasin. "Here," she said, handing them to Felicia. "Suck on one of these, and your throat will feel better. Are you all over the choking now?"

"Yes," Felicia whispered. "I'm okay."

"Good." Mrs. Goudy led her into a nearby bedroom. "Why don't you just rest for a few minutes, and then come down when you're ready? Take your time, dear. I'll tell your young man that you're all right." After patting Felicia's shoulder, she hurried back downstairs to her other guests.

Felicia wished she'd asked her about borrowing something to wear. She *had* to take off the dress. It was so tight she could barely move. Walking stiffly over to the mirror, which stood in a corner of the room, she looked into it, expecting to see the seams of the dress separating before her eyes. Her reflection looked back at her from the mirror, pale-faced and a little wild-eyed. The rows of lace scallops around her hips should have been pulled out of shape, the high collar should have been strangle-tight around her neck. But the dress — the dress hung smoothly, a perfect fit. It looked just as it had at the beginning of the evening when Mark had said she should be the queen of the ball.

What was wrong? She could *feel* its constriction, and even now it was getting tighter and tighter. Why didn't it *look* tight?

Frantically Felicia tore at the little buttons that held her captive inside the dress. She had to get it off. There was something awful about it. It seemed to have a life of its own. And that life was threatening *her* life.

She was surprised when the dress came off easily. She'd been prepared to cut it off if necessary. It fell to the floor with a sigh, and she stepped quickly away from it.

But what now? She *had* to get it back to Robin's hospital closet. She had to be free of it. She couldn't keep it overnight. What would it do to her, alone in her apartment? And she couldn't leave it there at the Goudy's house. They'd be sure to find it and think she'd lost her mind. And that surely would reflect somehow on Mark.

There was a bus line that ran just half a block from the campus of the divinity school. If she hurried, she could catch a bus, take the dress back to Robin's room, stop off at her own apartment to put on another dress, any dress, and return before anyone really missed her. She knew that was insane, that it would take an hour to do that. She could leave and phone, saying she was sick and had decided to go home but hadn't wanted to take Mark away from the party.

Quickly Felicia searched through the bedroom closet for something she could wear. She pulled out a pair of faded jeans and a shirt that must have belonged to Mrs. Goudy. She pulled them on. They were too large, but they felt good after the tightness of the dress. Seeing a visored cap on the closet shelf, she grabbed it, and jammed it on her head, poking her hair up under it. She'd be harder to recognize that way.

There was a blue zippered bag on the floor of the closet. She snatched that, too, and stuffed the dress into it. Then before she could think about it, she ran out into the hallway and peered down the stairs. She was weeping softly, and she brushed the tears away with the back of her hand.

Everyone was still eating. No one was in the entry hall.

Felicia's feet made no sound on the carpeted stairway. When she got to the polished wood floor of the entry hall, she slipped off her high-heeled shoes and poked them into the blue bag with the dress. Then she tiptoed toward the door.

But just as she opened it, Mrs. Goudy came from the dining room. She must have been going upstairs to check on her, Felicia thought.

"Who's there?" Mrs. Goudy called out. "Harry, somebody's been upstairs. Stop!"

Felicia ran from the house, slamming the door. Behind her she heard Mrs. Goudy yell, "Harry, he's got my blue bag. Somebody go after him!"

Chapter 8

Miss Feldstrom herself brought the letter to Robin. She and Cynthie came together, smiling tentatively as they peered into the room.

"Robin?" Cynthie said as if she were unsure about who was there, weighted down by the big casts.

"Hey, come on in." Robin tried to hoist herself up a little and was overwhelmed by a flash of pain. She must have grimaced, because Cynthie ran forward, looking alarmed.

"Robin," she said. "Don't sit up. Here, I'll fix your bed so you can see us better." She touched the button that raised up the head of the bed, watching Robin carefully to see that it didn't hurt her.

"Thanks, Dr. Wheeler," Robin said, trying to grin.

"I'll send you my bill," Cynthie said. "If you think you're wiped out now, wait till you get that."

All three of them laughed, lowering the tension level.

"How's everything at school?" Robin asked.

"Final exams coming up soon," Miss Feldstrom said. "Some people will do anything to get out of taking them." She rolled her eyes at Robin's casts.

Her joke fell a little flat, and she flushed. "Robin, I'm sorry. It's nothing to be facetious about."

Robin shrugged. "Being gloomy isn't going to help. Now, what brought the two of you here today, besides my magnetic personality?" Miss Feldstrom was mangling an envelope she'd brought with her. Robin figured it was for her, and if she didn't get it soon, it would be shredded.

"Oh." Miss Feldstrom looked at the envelope as if she'd just remembered she had it. "It's from the dance department at the university."

Robin wished she hadn't asked, and she turned her head away.

"Robin," Miss Feldstrom said. "They're offering you the dance scholarship. What's more, they'll hold it for you until you're ready to use it."

Robin turned back to them and stared silently at Miss Feldstrom. Would they hold the scholarship for a lifetime? Or would they let her come and dance in a wheelchair? Why had they even bothered to send it? Why had Miss Feldstrom bothered to bring it?

"Oh, good," she said bitterly. "I'll put taps on my wheels."

"You could coach some of the other students until. . . ." Miss Feldstrom's voice trailed off. "Until you're ready."

Robin knew she'd made Miss Feldstrom uncomfortable, but she couldn't help it. She felt panic rising inside her. What was going to happen to her now that she couldn't dance anymore? How was she going to spend all the years of her life? She looked at Miss Feldstrom, whose face crumpled.

"I've said the wrong thing again," Miss Feldstrom said.

"No, you didn't," Cynthie said fiercely. "Robin's going to dance again. She'll use that scholarship."

Robin wished she could believe her. She took a deep, quivering breath. "That was such a good night," she said. "The night of the dance concert, I mean."

Miss Feldstrom nodded, looking relieved that Robin wasn't going to wail out her despair. "You looked so lovely in that fringed dress. The people from the university were dazzled."

"You should have seen her the night of the prom," Cynthie said. "Dazzling to the tenth power."

"I heard your prom dress was spectacular," Miss Feldstrom said.

"Would you like to see it?" Robin suddenly had an urge to see it again herself. She pointed to the closet. "It's in there. Would you get it, Cynthie?"

"Fer sure, fer sure." Cynthie walked over and put her hands on the closet doorknob just as a businesslike nurse bustled into the room. Her name was Mrs. Hill. She filled in on the afternoon shift when Felicia wasn't there.

"Chow time," she said pleasantly. "Can I get a couple extra trays for you?" She looked at Cynthie and Miss Feldstrom.

"I just remembered an urgent appointment at the Golden Arches." Cynthie headed for the door. "I'll smuggle in a Big Mac for you if you want," she stage-whispered to Robin.

"I have to go, too," Miss Feldstrom said. "I have to make up a final exam." She laid the long white envelope she carried on Robin's bedside table.

She and Cynthie waved good-bye as they left.

Mrs. Hill smiled as she watched them go. "Best way to get rid of visitors is to offer them hospital food. Now, let's get you fed so you can take a little nap."

Robin was dancing alone on a brightly lit stage, pirouetting across the gleaming floor for an audience of one — Tyler. Tyler sat in the dim, cavernous auditorium and clapped his approval as she completed each maneuver of her intricate dance.

But then Miss Catherine was there, too. She sat in one of the far back balcony seats where Tyler couldn't see her.

"Give me my golden arm," she whispered, and suddenly she was in a front seat of the balcony. "Give me my golden arm," she cried out.

Why was Miss Catherine saying that? Robin didn't have her golden arm.

Now Miss Catherine was right on stage with her, tearing at the lacy, cream-colored dress

Robin wore. She couldn't get away from the tearing hands. Her feet had turned to lead. In the audience Tyler rose and called, "Robin! Are you all right?"

"Tyler," Robin cried, "help me! I can't move!"

She reached out to him, and he was there with her.

Miss Catherine was gone.

"Robin," Tyler said. "Wake up, honey. You're having a bad dream."

Waking, Robin saw where she was, and it was almost as bad as the dream. Her feet were indeed lead, or nearly so.

She pushed the white envelope from the University to the far end of her table and wept. Tyler held her close, whispering soft, gentle things as the sobs shook her body. He stayed until she was calm again.

They didn't talk about anything important. He told her what was going on at school in the closing days of the semester, and she told him about the daily routine at the hospital. They spoke of what they would do when she was well, the hikes they would take, the dances they would go to.

After Tyler left, Robin cried again because it was all make-believe, with no more substance than her dream. She wouldn't be hiking or dancing. That wasn't what Dr. Blake had said, exactly, but he'd showed her X rays of her feet. He'd explained about the hundreds of tiny bones in the feet and said jokingly that brain surgery was a snap compared to foot surgery.

There'd be more operations, he said. He didn't

know how many it would take to reconstruct her smashed feet. In the meantime, she'd have to wear the casts.

"The good news," he said, "is that we'll be sending you home soon."

Home in a wheelchair.

How long would Tyler stay around to push a wheelchair?

What had happened to Miss Catherine's beau after Rowena threw the acid that scarred her face? Had he stayed true to her? Or had he been repulsed by the ugly scar? Did he turn away from Catherine after her beauty was gone, leaving her to spend her life alone?

Gabrielle came about twenty minutes after Tyler left. She entered the room pink-cheeked, saying she'd been talking to Tyler in the hospital lobby.

"He said you'd had a bad dream." She pulled a chair close to the bed and sat down. "Was it about the accident?"

"It was weird," Robin said. "Miss Catherine was in it, and she kept saying, 'Give me my golden arm.'"

Gabrielle laughed. "That's from the old ghost story Daddy used to tell us. Remember? The one where the man steals a golden arm from a corpse and then the dead guy follows him all over asking for it?"

Now Robin remembered. It made the dream all the more terrifying.

"Miss Catherine's back, by the way." Gabby stood up and paced over to the window where she stood for a moment, looking out. "She called yesterday to see when you were coming to work. I told her what happened to you. She didn't ask about the dress, so I guess she was more concerned about you than it."

Robin's heart jumped. "You didn't say anything about it, did you? I mean, I think it would be better if I explained about the damage myself."

"I didn't mention it, Robbie." She gave Robin a curious look. "What's the big deal anyway?"

Robin took a deep breath to smooth out her voice. "Well, you know, don't you, that it got torn a little in the accident? I just want to have it all fixed before I tell Miss Catherine about it." Fervently she wished she'd taken Gabrielle into her confidence before Miss Catherine had come back. Maybe Gabby could have sneaked it back up to its hiding place in the attic. She knew Miss Catherine was going to be furious. It was going to be a long time before Robin could walk up those stairs — if ever.

Gabby was stirring around in the duffel-sized purse she always carried. "Aha," she said, triumphantly holding up a tiny sewing kit. "Like the Boy Scouts, I'm always prepared. Why don't I leave this and you can stitch up the tears sometime when you don't have anything else to do?" She grinned, as if Robin had such a full social life that it would be hard to find time.

"Better still," Robin said, "why don't you sew it up? You have the talented fingers. All my talents are in my . . . feet." Her voice dropped off.

Gabby glanced out of the window again, then smiled. "Better even than that, I'll take it home and do it. Otherwise I'll make you listen to the story of Mozart's love life while I work."

Gabby liked to read biographies of her favorite composers and was always complaining that nobody but Tyler ever wanted to hear about the things she'd read.

Robin gave a big, fake sigh. "Okay, I'll do it myself. Just bring it here. I might as well do it right now. Or maybe I'll get Felicia to do it. She's my nurse most afternoons and evenings. She offered to do it a couple of nights ago." She didn't want Gabby to take it home. She didn't want Gabby sewing it, touching it.

Gabby walked over to the narrow closet and opened the door. "Okay," she said, "give me a clue about where to find it."

"Cut it out, Gab. Just bring it here."

Gabby stepped aside so Robin could see into the bare closet. "It's not here, Robbie."

The dress *couldn't* be gone. But Robin could see with her own eyes that it was, and no amount of staring into the closet was going to make it materialize.

Her mouth went dry. "Call the nurse," she whispered.

Gabby hurried to her bedside. "Are you okay, Robbie? You don't look so good."

"I'm okay." She made an effort to control herself. "Just call the nurse. I'm sure somebody took the dress to a safer place."

Gabby left the room in search of the nurse. Robin continued to stare at the empty closet. She'd dreamed she saw somebody take the dress out of the closet a few days before. Who was it? What was it she'd said?

Had it been more than a dream?

Robin couldn't remember. She'd been so full of medication for pain that her memory was blurred.

Gabby came back with Mrs. Hill. "Is something wrong, Robin?" she asked.

"I just want to know where my dress is," Robin said.

"Oh, we always send the patients' clothes home with relatives," Mrs. Hill said cheerfully. "Or if there's some reason they want them here, we leave them in the closet." She looked into the open compartment. "Your dress must have gone home."

Both Robin and Gabrielle shook their heads.

"Well, I'll go see where it is. Whoever took it away must have left a notation." Nurse Hill went out, leaving the impression that if the dress existed, she'd find it.

Robin felt weak and so weary. She tried again to remember who it was who had held the dress up to look at it. But it was all too foggy. A dream, the way the dancing had been a dream.

Mrs. Hill returned. "There's no record of anyone moving your dress, Robin. But I did find out that Felicia Martin was on duty the night you were brought in. She must have put the dress somewhere. We'll find out when she comes in tomorrow." That settled, Nurse Hill went out again.

Gabby didn't stay much longer. She seemed

nervous. Fidgety. As if someone was waiting outside for her.

Tyler? Was Tyler waiting to drive her home?

But Gabby wouldn't do that to her. She wouldn't flirt with Tyler while Robin was helpless. Would she?

"Gabby," Robin said. But with a smile and a wave, Gabby ran out of the room.

"Wait," Robin called.

But Gabby was gone. Gone to Tyler?

"Don't be paranoid," Robin said aloud to herself. "She's my sister." Somehow that made her feel better.

She picked up the letter Miss Feldstrom had left and looked at it briefly, then dropped it into the wastebasket at the side of her bed.

She slept again. She was running this time, not dancing. She was running down a long corridor, with doors on each side. They were all closed. Then the corridor slanted upwards, and Robin ran until her heart wanted to leap out of her body. She came to Miss Catherine's attic, to the door of the dark little closet under the eaves. As she stood panting, the door creaked open. Miss Catherine was there, standing among the cobwebs, the right side of her face smiling. She reached out for Robin, whose feet suddenly felt as if they were nailed to the floor.

"Robin," she said, "give me my golden arm."

The the scar on her face faded, to be replaced by a dark red splotch, which covered her entire left cheek, and Robin knew that it was Rowena there in the dismal closet.

Rowena, who was criminally insane.

Chapter 9

Felicia didn't stop to put her shoes on again. She could run better in her stocking feet anyway. If she was lucky, the bus would be there at the edge of the small campus, and she could get right on it. She'd take the dress back to the hospital and somehow get it into the closet in Robin's room. Surely Robin would be asleep by now, and she could just tiptoe in there and leave it.

But then what would she do? What reason could she give for leaving the party?

The night air was making her more rational. Suddenly the whole thing didn't sound like such a good idea any more. Maybe she should just go back and make up some story. What kind of story? What possible explanation could there be for her behavior?

What would she say to Mark? Plead insanity maybe? He'd probably believe it if she told him about the dress, about the way it had grown tighter and tighter.

She ran on.

Far behind her, she heard pounding footsteps. "Stop!" somebody yelled. Mark?

She ran faster, aware of small stones on the sidewalk that hurt her feet but not caring. The bus was coming down the street. It would pull into the bus stop at just about the same time as she arrived.

The bus pulled up and stopped. The door hissed open. She sprang aboard without even slowing down.

The bus driver grinned. "The cops after you, girlie?"

Felicia looked at him, startled.

"Just kidding," he said. He glanced at the two dollar bills she thrust at him. "I don't make change."

She wasn't sure what the fare was. "Keep it." She dropped both bills into his hand and went to the back of the bus where she collapsed onto a seat. There were only a few other passengers, but she wanted to be back there, alone, where she could think. The bus was in semi-darkness. One of the overhead lights was out, and another one kept flickering on and off, making the movements of the passengers look jerky, like an old-time movie. It gave Felicia an eerie, disoriented feeling, but she hoped the darkness hid her frightened eyes and tear-streaked face.

What was she going to do now? Whatever she did, she was in trouble. Why hadn't she just had Mark take her home? But the dress had been strangling her. She'd *had* to get it off. She stared at the blue zippered bag that she held on her lap. Could it have been her imagination? How could anything as beautiful as that dress be evil?

Sliding the zipper open, she peered inside. The dress lay there, crumpled and innocent in the flickering light. Somehow she'd expected it to glimmer with some devilish light of its own.

Surely she had imagined the whole thing. Maybe what she should do was get off the bus, change into the dress, return to Dean Goudy's house, sneak up the back stairs, and come downstairs again as if nothing had happened. She might even say she'd heard somebody stirring around in the next room. Maybe she'd even glimpsed a man running off with the blue zippered bag.

That was crazy. She'd never be able to pull it off. But she had to do something. Whoever had pursued her had probably gone back to the Goudy's house and called the police. He'd probably reported that the burglar had got on the bus.

She should get off. It wasn't much farther to the hospital. She could walk the rest of the way along the dark streets and return the dress. Then she could change into the spare uniform she kept in her locker and throw the shirt and jeans in a trash can.

She yanked the cap off her head and dropped it out of the half-open window. The police would be looking for a man with a cap, not a girl with long black hair.

Before she pulled the cord for the bus to stop, she felt in the bag for her shoes. She'd better put them on so she could get off with some dignity and save her feet, too.

She found only one. Alarmed, she felt around

for the other one. It was at the bottom of the bag. But there was something else there, too. Her groping fingers fastened around it and she pulled it out.

It was a small velvet pouch, the kind you put jewelry in when you're going on a trip. And it wasn't empty.

With trembling hands, Felicia opened the pouch. Inside was a strand of pearls and a pair of earrings. She touched the pearls. They felt slightly rough. These were *not* costume jewelry pearls. They were real. They were expensive.

Felicia groaned. What had she done? She was a thief twice over, now. First the dress, then the jewelry, to say nothing of the clothes and the blue bag.

She closed the pouch quickly and shoved it back into the blue bag with the dress and her shoes. After zipping it shut, she put the bag under her seat, as if by getting it out of her sight she could forget it existed.

What was she going to do? What *could* she do now?

She stayed on the bus. It stopped every few blocks, and its doors hissed open to let people on and off. It passed the hospital, but still she stayed, ducking her head, hiding her face, wondering if her guilt showed.

Integrity, Dean Goudy had said. That was a quality he admired. She'd ruined Mark. Dean Goudy would never give a recommendation to anyone whose girlfriend stole his wife's jewelry.

Even if she put on the dress and ran back now, she could never take the blue bag with her because they'd know she'd taken it. She couldn't walk into the hospital with it, either.

She could say she'd wrestled it away from the burglar. No, they'd never believe that. Tears were running down her face again, and she moaned.

The bus stopped again, and somebody got on. She felt the vibration of feet as they came running to the back of the bus.

"Felicia!"

She looked up. It was Mark. Mark and another man from the party. Mark looked totally bewildered.

"Hey, you guys," the bus driver yelled. "You gotta pay if you're gonna ride."

"Keep your shirt on," the man with Mark said. "We're getting off again. Mark and I just came after somebody."

The bus driver stood up. "These guys bothering you, girlie?"

"No!" Felicia said. "They're friends of mine." She stood up, too. "We're just playing a game," she said desperately.

"How about letting me in on the rules?" the bus driver grumbled. "Get off if you're gonna. I gotta keep this thing rolling."

Numbly, Felicia followed Mark and the other man off the bus. The bus shooshed off, and she saw Mark's car standing on the other side of the street, its front doors open as if its occupants had gotten out in a hurry.

"Felicia," Mark said. "*What's* going on? Maybe you should let *me* in on the rules of this game, too."

"I just said that for the driver's benefit." Felicia's voice was almost a whisper.

"Well, what happened? Bill and I came after the man who ran out of Dean Goudy's house and we saw him get on the bus. We got my car and followed — and we find you, Felicia." Mark shook his head in disbelief. "Where's your dress?"

The dress! It was in the bag, which was still on the bus. Felicia put out her hand to touch Mark's arm. "Mark. Listen, *please*."

She stopped. If she told him where the bag was, they'd know she'd taken it. They'd catch the bus at the next stop and get it. They'd take it back to Dean and Mrs. Goudy, and she'd be charged with the theft of the jewelry. Then Robin would report her dress missing and that would be traced to Felicia, too.

"Mark. The man with the cap," she said breathlessly. Thank goodness she'd had the sense to throw the cap away. "*He* took it. He *made* me take the dress off at the house and he put it in a blue bag that he found in a closet."

"That's the bag Mrs. Goudy saw," Mark said. "What happened to the guy who took it?" He looked in the direction the bus had gone.

"He got off a couple stops back," Felicia said quickly.

Oh, why had she said that? They could check that with the driver. He might not remember everybody who got off, but he would remember that she'd gotten on alone. With the bag. He'd noticed her when she'd gotten on and had even spoken to her.

Bill gave her a skeptical look. "Why didn't you tell the driver to call the police *then*?" he asked.

"I was too scared," Felicia said. "He *made* me come with him. He said he'd hurt me if I didn't come. He threatened all sorts of awful things. I didn't dare call out or anything. I just did what he said. I'm sorry that he got away. But I was afraid. See, I'm still shaking." Her words raced out of her mouth, one falling over the other.

"Oh, sweetheart." Mark took her in his arms. "What an awful experience."

The shaking was real. So were the tears that fell from Felicia's eyes and the anguish that was in her voice. But they were for a different reason than Mark thought.

She put her head on his shoulder and let him stroke her hair, soothing her as she cried. She'd never loved him as much as she did at that moment when he trusted her unquestioningly. Her heart broke at the thought of betraying that trust.

"It was horrible," she said against his shoulder. "He took me totally by surprise. I wasn't thinking clearly, or I'd have yelled for help."

"We saw only one person running from the house," Bill said.

Why didn't he just keep quiet? "I'm wearing dark clothes," Felicia said. "He told me to run in the shadows. He made me go along with him."

"Did he have a gun?" Bill asked.

"Cool it," Mark said. "She can answer all the questions when we get back to the house. Dean Goudy has probably called the police by now."

The police! What did they do to you for lying to the police? Mentally, Felicia added perjury to her list of crimes.

But what else could she do?

The police were polite. That made it easier to lie. Felicia told her story of the intruder upstairs. She almost was beginning to believe it. She said she'd been feeling sick from a choking episode, which Mrs. Goudy verified. The man, who'd worn a cap, had been hiding in a closet and had demanded that she take off her obviously expensive dress, which he stuffed into a blue bag along with some other things.

"Your shoes, too?" the taller of the policeman asked.

"Yes," Felicia said smoothly. "I guess he didn't want me to make noise when we went downstairs."

The policeman nodded. Felicia congratulated herself on her adroit answer.

The police called the bus company and asked to be put in touch with the driver of Bus No. 6 on the Reynolds Avenue line. The bus office called him on their radio hookup, and the policeman who was doing the talking asked if he remembered two people getting on at the campus stop, a girl in jeans and a man dressed in dark clothes and a cap.

Felicia sat rigidly, listening.

The officer reported that the bus driver said he remembered the girl because she'd been so breathless. He didn't remember a guy, but there were people getting on and off all the time so he couldn't say for sure. The girl carried a blue bag, he said. She'd paid double fare. And yes, somewhere somebody wearing a cap had gotten on. It could have been there.

Felicia nodded. "He made me carry the bag when we got on the bus. He said it looked like the kind of bag a woman would carry, so it would look less suspicious if I had it. And I gave the driver two dollars. The driver remembered."

The policeman asked the bus driver to check to see if the bag might still be on the bus.

Felicia held her breath. If it was there, she could say the thief must have left it when he got off. She hadn't seen what he did with it after he took it from her. She could say that. Oh, what was going to happen to her? Would she be believed?

But after a few minutes passed, long enough for the driver to pull to a stop and search the bus, the policeman reported that he said the bag wasn't on board.

Then where was it? Who had taken it? Felicia's head was spinning with questions that were unanswered. After a few more questions, the police left.

Felicia felt nothing but relief. It occurred to her that she ought to feel overwhelmed with guilt. Instead, she congratulated herself that so far she'd pulled it off. She'd convinced them all that she'd been abducted by a shadowy crook who made off with her dress and Mrs. Goudy's jewelry. And there was nothing to connect her to the dress at the hospital. It was dangerous to leave valuable possessions in the closets at the hospital. Almost anyone could wander in and take them, the same way as someone had taken the bag with the dress inside from the bus. She hoped that whoever had it would take it far, far away, where she'd never have to see it again.

Mark stayed a while when he took her home to her apartment.

"You've had a rough week," he said. "Do you think you'll be able to sleep?"

"I think so," she said. "I'm working tomorrow to make up for taking yesterday off, but I'm sure I'll be able to drift off for a while at least."

"I'll stay here on the sofa if you'd like me to," Mark offered. "This whole thing might hit you in the middle of the night."

That's what Felicia was afraid of. Sometimes she talked in her sleep, especially after something traumatic happened.

"You're sweet for offering," she said. "But really, I'll be fine."

Mark kissed her tenderly and went to the door. "By the way," he said, "the Dean thinks you're a real trooper. And so do I."

Felicia smiled. She couldn't believe things had worked out so well. Too well, actually. Somewhere there had to be a pit waiting for her. Sometime she would fall in and struggle to get out again. Suddenly she felt as if her web of lies was tightening around her the same way the dress had.

Chapter 10

Nicole Eckhart was only mildly curious when her foot bumped against something under her bus seat. Actually, it almost seemed as if whatever it was had made the movement that brought her foot in contact with it. She'd thought maybe it was a dog someone had smuggled aboard, or a stowaway cat.

But when she looked under the seat, she saw a blue zippered bag, like the kind her brother carried his basketball uniform and shoes in, to and from school. Probably someone had forgotten it there on the bus.

She pulled the bag from under the seat, and holding it gingerly, expecting to see — and smell — some moldy sneakers and dirty gym socks, she unzipped it.

She couldn't believe her eyes. Inside the bag was a dress, a delicate, lacy, cream-colored dress that fairly lit up the dark bag. From what she could see, it was her dream dress, the kind that projected an image of a beautiful young woman, not a teenage girl. The kind that would catch the eye of. . . . No, that was her secret. She wasn't even going to think his name. That might jinx whatever fate it was that had sent her the dress. She touched the dress gently and it seemed to cling to her fingers.

Nicole believed in fate. Hadn't her astrological forecast that very morning said that the outlook for the fulfillment of a cherished desire was favorable that day? *Take advantage of opportunities that may arise*, it advised. She'd thought when she read it that it had something to do with the last phase of the academic decathlon she was taking part in the next day, the competition that required mental gymnastics rather than physical. She and the other team members from Tullidge High would be competing with other top teams of their state in ten academic events. There would be stiff competition, and Nicole and the rest of her team would need all the help they could get.

But now she knew the astrological forecast meant just what it said. *Today*. Today, this evening, was the reception for the decathlon participants, and that was when she'd hoped. . . . No, don't think about it, she told herself. Just let it come. The whole night lay ahead, a tantalizing, magical, anything-could-happen night. The dress, which she knew without thinking that she would wear, would make the night magical. She and the others would be staying in the dorms at the university, where the decathlon was to be held, so her mother wasn't around to worry if she wasn't in by midnight. Of course, there'd be curfew rules, since everyone needed to bone up on this year's decathlon subjects before the next day. But if . . . no, don't write the script ahead of time, she cautioned herself.

She closed the blue zippered bag, wondering if anybody else had seen her pull it from under her seat. Probably not. Her teammates John and Tanya were too involved in one another to notice anything she did or didn't do. She hoped they would come out of their blue fog tomorrow, long enough to make a good showing in the decathlon. For them it was just an interesting sideline in their lives, the main advantage being that they were doing it together. Whether they made a good showing or not wasn't going to change their lives a whole lot.

For Nicole, it was her big chance. She wasn't really beautiful, like Tanya, although her red hair and blue eyes were attractive. She wasn't athletic or musically gifted or rich. All she had going for her was her brain, her quick, retentive brain that could absorb, process, and give back information like a computer. Better than a computer, since she didn't have to depend on the limitations of the programmer. Mr. Waring, their decathlon team coach, was always saying that he wished they could invent a printer to hook up to Nicole's brain and they'd have the best computer in the business. The other team members laughingly agreed.

Was that how they regarded her? As a machine?

They wouldn't after they saw her in the dress. The beautiful lacy dress that she knew was glowing in the blue bag, beckoning to her, calling to her. And tomorrow they'd see her differently, too, remembering the new Nicole they'd see tonight in the lace dress. Mr. Waring would be so proud when she led her team to victory. Mr. Waring was the best academic coach in the state. Even though Tullidge High was one of the smallest schools involved, their team was holding its own against all competitors.

She hoped Mr. Waring hadn't seen her lift the bag from under her seat. But he probably hadn't even looked around, once he'd seen that she was comfortably settled back there by herself in the spot she'd chosen, far away from the others, in the dark recesses of the bus. She'd said she needed to concentrate, but the truth was, she'd wanted to dream without having to talk to anybody. Just to keep up the pretense, she had kept an open book on her lap and had been dreamily looking at it when her feet had touched the blue bag under her seat.

Mr. Waring was sitting with Bryan Bentley, whose brown hair was all spiky from the finger-combings he gave it while he studied. Bryan was something of a football jock, and he had to study harder than the others to stay on the team. But once he learned a thing, he never forgot it, so it was just a matter of fierce study.

He turned now and looked back at Nicole. "Hey, Nicole," he called, "how about handling any geography questions that come at us? I can't even remember whether Lansing is the capital of Iowa or Idaho."

"Oboy," she said. "Are we in trouble!"

He was just teasing, and she grinned at him,

knowing full well that any geography questions that came up he would be able to handle.

Mr. Waring and John and Tanya all turned to smile at her. Sometimes they called her "Encyclopedia Eckhart," because she could fill in all the gaps they didn't know in the physical and social sciences, as well as literature and, most of the time, math, too.

They all made some kind of remark to her, and she clutched the blue zippered bag close against her, marveling at the fate which had brought them all together. She and Bryan were the only ones who'd grown up in the town of Tullidge. The others had all come from elsewhere, Mr. Waring most recently. He'd come there after his wife and baby daughter had been killed in a freak accident. It was fate that had brought them together, and fate that had put them on the bus that day rather than coming in Mr. Waring's battered station wagon, whose battery had given out at the last moment. There hadn't been room for them in the other car with the rest of the team members and alternates. And they didn't have time to recruit another car. So they'd had to come here to Forest Dale on the Greyhound, and at the bus station they'd gotten on the city bus, just so she could find the dress in the blue zippered bag. Fate provided the opportunity she needed.

She knew without even pulling it out of the bag that the dress would fit her. She'd already checked the shoes that were in the bag, too. They were just her size. It was all unbelievable.

It was fate that she'd come to sit on the seat under which the bag was. It was as if the dress had been calling out to her. Maybe the bag *had* actually moved over to bump her foot. She'd wanted so desperately to show *him* tonight that she was a warm and desirable woman. More than just a high school girl. More than just a machine. A brain *plus* everything else a person like him would want.

The bus driver had been talking on his two-way radio, but Nicole was too far away to hear what the incoming voice was saying. She sensed, however, that it might have something to do with the blue bag.

As the bus jolted to a stop, she put the bag back on the floor, pushing it against the side of the bus; then she moved her own suitcase to cover it, putting her bookpack on top of everything.

The bus driver hoisted himself from his seat and yelled, "Will you all take a look under your seats and see if there is a blue zippered bag there? Somebody's looking for it. She says she left it on this bus when she got off several miles back."

Nicole's heart shifted guiltily. Some poor girl must be devastated about losing that dress. But why had she stuffed it in a bag like that? If it was that important to her, she should have packed it better. She should have taken care of it, the way Nicole would have.

Even so, Nicole knew she should turn it in. After all, it belonged to somebody else, somebody who remembered where she'd left it. Somebody who wanted it back.

But Nicole *needed* it. She could turn it in later, saying she'd found it on the bus. Nobody need ever know that she hadn't got off *before* the driver made his announcement about the bag. The owner would get her dress back eventually. But not yet.

All the people on the bus ducked down to peer under their seats. The bus driver came down the aisle, bending over to scan the floor himself.

"The girl says she was near the back of the bus," he said when he got to Nicole. "Did you see anything back here?"

Nicole shook her head. "I've got my own stuff here, but I can't see anything under the seat." She leaned over to look.

The bus driver shrugged. "Probably somebody already took it. I can't keep track of everything that goes on. I've got a bus to drive." He kept on muttering as he returned to his seat. Nicole heard him report that the blue zippered bag was not aboard his bus.

She felt hot as the bus started up again. Perspiration trickled down her back, and her hands were sweaty. Perhaps even now she should grab the bag and take it to the driver, saying she'd located it in a dark corner.

No, the dress had been *sent* to her because she needed it so desperately. The skirt and blouse she had in her old suitcase wouldn't do for tonight. She'd asked her mother for a new dress for this special occasion, this reception for all the participants in the final phase of the decathlon, but of course her mother had just sighed and said Nicole knew as well as she did that her father was still out of work and there was no money.

The reception was to be a dress-up event.

Tanya had a special dress, but Tanya had special dresses for everything. She didn't even *need* special dresses because she had John, who saw her with eyes full of love no matter how she was dressed.

Nicole made no move to take the bag up to the driver. No. It was her dress for the night.

She solved the problem of how to get the blue bag off the bus by shoving it inside her suitcase. There wasn't much else in the suitcase, except the skirt and blouse she'd planned to wear that night and another set for the decathlon events the next day.

Nicole and Tanya were sharing a room at the dorm on the university campus where the decathlon was being held. Nicole didn't want to open the suitcase in front of Tanya, but that wasn't a problem. Tanya stayed in the room only long enough to dump her things, then left to be with John, saying she'd be back in time to dress for the dinner and reception at the Student Union.

Now Nicole could take the dress out and smooth away the wrinkles. She could rejoice in the fate that brought it to her and think about what it, in turn, would bring in the future.

Opening the blue zippered bag, she tenderly lifted out the dress and held it up. It was even more beautiful than she'd imagined, and there were amazingly few wrinkles, nothing that wouldn't disappear if she hung it in the bathroom while she showered.

Quickly she took off her school clothes and tried

on the dress. Its lacy scallops whispered down over her body, and the high collar caressed her neck. The long sleeves hid her freckled arms, and the soft, creamy color softened the redness of her hair.

Just as she'd known, it fit to perfection. It clung to her body, making her feel wrapped in warmth.

She dug into the blue bag again to get the shoes, which fate had also so thoughtfully provided.

When she reached in, she felt something else besides the shoes. Something soft. Velvet. She pulled it out and saw that it was a little bag with a drawstring closing.

There was something inside.

She opened the bag and poured its contents out onto the bed.

Jewelry! A string of pearls. Some pearl earrings. A pearl ring.

Well! When fate decided to dress her up, it was a virtual fairy godmother.

Humming happily, she put the pearls around her neck and slipped the ring on her finger. Perfect! And the earrings. Now she knew why she'd had the impulse to have her ears pierced just a month before. All in preparation for this night. She took out the little gold earrings she'd been wearing and put in the pearls, wondering all the while if they were real.

The dress, the pearls, the shoes—they all seemed to have been made for one another. For her!

She walked around the small dorm room, watching herself in the mirrors of the twin dressers. Who'd ever guess that this was plain old Nicole Eckhart, who dazzled people with her brain and would now dazzle them with her beauty?

What was that on her left cheek? It looked as if she had a mud pack on that side of her face. But when she went to the mirror for a closer look, the odd marking was gone. They needed to put a new mirror in the dorm room. This one played tricks with the light.

She wobbled a little on the high heels of the ivory pumps as she backed away from the mirror. She wasn't used to wearing spiky heels. But oh, what they did for her legs! She doubted if Bryan or Mr. Waring or the others had ever even noticed that she *had* legs since she generally wore flats or tennies with her jeans or skirts.

She looked at her watch. There was just time for a quick shower before the dinner. She'd better hurry. She didn't want Tanya to come in while she was wearing the dress. In fact, she wanted to get dressed and go to the Student Union building before Tanya came. She didn't want to go with Tanya. She wanted to go alone, with nothing to detract from her and the lovely dress when *he* saw her.

Tanya came while Nicole was in the shower.

"Wait for me," Tanya said as Nicole came out wrapped in a towel. "I'll shower, and then we'll go out together."

Since Tanya had turned on some loud music

from a tape deck she'd brought, it was easy for Nicole to pretend she hadn't heard. Dressing swiftly in the lace dress while Tanya was in the shower, she hurried from the dorm room.

It wasn't until she was on the shady walkway leading to the Student Union that she had some doubts about wearing the dress and jewelry. What if they belonged to a girl who was also taking part in the decathlon? What if the owner was there in the dining room, watching as Nicole entered?

Nicole hesitated only briefly. The dress rustled enchantingly as she hurried on her way. Out of the corner of her eye she could see girls turning to look at her.

"Gorgeous dress," one of them murmured.

Nicole felt like singing out with happiness, but instead she concentrated on walking carefully on the high heels.

The Student Union building was beautiful. Potted palms decorated the large entryway. The palms were only plastic, but they looked real and gave the whole place a kind of exotic air. The marble floors gleamed. Soft lights lit up the dining room, which was through a wide doorway to her right. Beside the doorway was a tall pedestal on which perched a bust of a man with flowing hair and a large mustache. Attached to the pedestal was a sign that said, "Welcome, Einsteins of the future!"

Maybe she *was* an Einstein of the future. But right now she was very content to be in the present.

Suddenly she wasn't worried anymore about the owner of the dress being there. The benefits were stacked high against the possible risk. After all, hadn't her horoscope for the day advised, *Take advantage of opportunities that may arise?*

Chapter 11

Nicole stood for just a moment by the bust of Einstein before entering the dining room. Just for luck she reached out a hand and touched the rough stone of the pedestal, which turned out to be not stone at all but just some kind of heavy, molded plastic. Touching things was a habit she'd had since childhood, when she believed in magic and didn't want to miss touching something that might send good luck her way.

Taking a deep breath, she walked carefully toward the table where John, Bryan, and Mr. Waring sat watching her. She still felt a little wobbly in the high-heeled pumps, and she didn't want to ruin her entrance by twisting an ankle and falling on her face. She might as well be wearing arch-support shoes for all the impression she'd make then. So she took small, almost stiff steps, aware all the time that walking that way made her hips sway the way Tanya's did.

John, Bryan, and Mr. Waring all stood up as they watched her coming, as if she were a queen.

She wouldn't have been surprised if they'd all bowed.

"Wow, Nicole," John breathed. "You sure look different."

Bryan merely nodded, and Nicole saw his Adam's apple bob up and down as he swallowed whatever he'd been nibbling on. Apparently it went down the wrong way because he suddenly choked and began coughing. John and Mr. Waring had to thump him on the back.

"Gosh, Nicole," he said with a grin when he could talk. "Walk in like that tomorrow, and we'll win the decathlon without ever saying a word."

The three guys laughed, and Nicole joined them.

Trying for nonchalance, she said, "For a minute I thought I'd get to practice the Heimlich Maneuver we've been learning about."

"If you'll practice some mouth-to-mouth resuscitation, I'll be glad to choke again." Bryan posed as if he were about to drop to the floor.

Mr. Waring hadn't said anything. He didn't need to. It was all in his eyes. At last he was seeing more than Nicole Eckhart, Girl Computer.

Now she could admit it to herself. She was in love with Mr. Waring. In love with *Steve*, although she had never called him by that name. She'd thought it was hopeless, but from the way Mr. Waring was looking at her now, she felt anything was possible. And all because of the dress.

Nicole put out a hand to stop Bryan from sinking all the way to the floor, which he was about to do. "Don't do it, dahling," she drawled. "I really wouldn't want to smear my lipstick."

The three men laughed again, and Nicole's heart bumped happily inside her chest. Was that all it took, just being dressed right, to make her feel like the witty, popular woman she'd always dreamed of being?

"Nicole." Mr. Waring was finally speaking. "Nicole, you've taken our collective breath away. We already knew you were the brainiest girl in the room, but now we see that you're the most beautiful, too."

"How come you've kept it a secret for so long?" Bryan blurted out, and everyone laughed again.

"What's the joke?" Tanya asked, arriving just as the laughter was dying down. She looked at John, then glanced at Bryan, Mr. Waring, and last of all, Nicole, before returning her gaze to John. Then, in a classic double-take, her eyes came back to Nicole. "Nicole, for heaven's sake — is that you?"

Nicole raised her nose in fake offense. "Well, I must say it's not very flattering to have everybody be so surprised. On a regular day I must look like Hecate." She thought that was especially appropriate since one of the literary works they'd been instructed to study for the decathlon was Shakespeare's *Macbeth*, in which Hecate was the queen of the witches.

The others quickly assured her that this was just such a change from her usual blue jeans that they couldn't quite get used to it. She loved it. She loved being beautiful. She loved being the center of attention. She loved the dress. And most of all, she loved the way Mr. Waring kept looking at her as if he'd never seen her before. He'd looked at her with admiration before, when she'd been able to snap out the right answers to the questions in the practice rounds of the decathlon. But not this way.

Other people were looking at her, too. She had a hunch she wasn't going to sit on the sidelines at the short dance that would come after the dinner and reception; afterwards they would all go to their rooms to cram for the next day. But the only one she really wanted to dance with was Mr. Waring. She wondered if he'd ask her.

"Everybody be seated," somebody said over a mike. "Dinner is about to be served."

Mr. Waring stepped over to pull Nicole's chair out for her, almost colliding with Bryan, who had the same idea. Nicole smiled at both of them. "Thank you," she said, happy that Mr. Waring was going to sit on her left. That was her best profile.

She wished she'd had time to run down to the student store she'd seen on the way to the dorm and see if they'd had some exotic perfume. Tanya always wore White Shoulders. Maybe she could have borrowed a whiff of that. But actually, there seemed to be just a hint of scent coming from the dress itself, something fresh and flowery. Something that made her feel a little dizzy. Nicole didn't recognize it, but it seemed appropriate for the dress's lacy perfection. Its sweetness matched the sweetness of the dress.

It made Nicole think about the girl who had last worn the dress, and again she experienced a moment of uneasiness. She looked around, half expecting to see a pair of baleful eyes glaring at her, or perhaps an angry girl swooping down to snatch the dress right off her back.

But all she saw were admiring, or envious, glances.

"Why didn't you wait for me, Nicole?" Tanya asked, spreading her napkin on her lap. "I hurried through my shower so you wouldn't have to wait so long, but you were already gone."

She seemed a little miffed. Before Nicole could open her mouth, John said, "You wouldn't have wanted to come in with Nicole. She was enough to knock a guy off his feet, walking in alone the way she did."

There was a moment of silence. Nicole wished John had stated things a little more tactfully. Tanya's face was reddening.

"I don't suppose anybody wants to talk about the cultural contributions of the New England states during the nineteenth century?" Mr. Waring asked. "Just to brush up for the history part of the decathlon."

That relaxed the tension a little, and Nicole loved him all the more for trying to cover up John's blunder.

But John wasn't finished. "What I meant was, if the *two* of you had come in at the same time, every guy in the room would have dropped dead."

Everybody at the table laughed, but the damage had already been done. Tanya gave Nicole a look that said, "Keep away from my guy," then concentrated on eating her chicken Kiev as if it were the most interesting food she'd ever encountered. John tried to include her in the conversation that Mr. Waring kept going, but Tanya scarcely looked up.

Nicole began to understand why some beautiful girls are not particularly well liked by other girls.

Truly, Nicole felt as if she were living in a dream. The Student Union, where the dinner and reception were being held, wasn't a fancy hotel, but to Nicole's inexperienced eyes it was glamorous enough, especially when she thought about it being on the campus of an important university. And there she sat, made beautiful and confident by the lacy dress. She'd never thought of herself as a good conversationalist, but tonight there seemed no end of things to say, things that sparked responses from the three men and made them laugh. Tanya didn't join in, but after a while Nicole stopped worrying about that. Maybe now Tanya would understand how she, Nicole, sometimes felt when Tanya captivated everyone in sight with her brains and beauty and Nicole sat silent.

After the dinner there were speeches, all praising the students and complimenting them on being representatives of their various schools. There were a few cautions about how they should comport themselves since what they did would reflect on their schools, but it was all done good-naturedly. There was also advice that they shouldn't stay up too late studying and be red-eyed and addle-brained for the final competitions the next day.

"I'll sleep better knowing we have Nicole on our side," Bryan said.

John laughed and murmured, "Me, too," and Mr. Waring looked at her with shining eyes.

Tanya glowered at her plate. She wasn't going to be much help the next day if she was all tied up with jealousy and anger.

"I can't do anything without Tanya," Nicole said. "We're a team. We're all a team." She turned to Mr. Waring. "How about it, Coach? Want to give a little last-minute drill? Now's the time to talk about the first law of thermodynamics."

Mr. Waring smiled. "Hey, you guys," he said softly. "You're the greatest. Each one of you has a contribution to make. I believe in you." He looked at each one, his glance lingering for a moment on Nicole. "No drills. It's all in your heads already. As long as you don't spring any leaks, you'll take Tullidge High to the top."

Even Tanya raised her head to cheer with the rest of them. Inspired by their enthusiasm, other groups began cheering.

Let them cheer, Nicole thought. They don't have a chance. After this magical night, she knew that anything could happen. She knew that her team could very well take top honors. They'd do it for Mr. Waring. For Steve.

Before the reception and dance began, Tanya asked Nicole if she'd like to accompany her to the women's room. It was while they were both repairing their lipstick that Tanya said, "That's a fabulous dress, Nicole. Where did you get it?"

The question surprised Nicole. She stammered out something about borrowing it from a cousin. Tanya knew her family would never have been able to afford anything like that.

"I'll only be wearing it this once," Nicole said, making her voice sound mournful. "My cousin never loans it more than once to the same person." That would explain why she wouldn't be showing up in it again. "She says one night in a dress like this is all a girl needs to realize her dreams."

Tanya was silent for a moment. Then she said, "Wasn't that odd about somebody leaving a bag on the bus? I wonder what was in it."

Did she suspect something? How could she? She hadn't even seen the blue bag. Or had she perhaps been snooping while Nicole was in the shower? Tanya didn't say anything further as they went back to their table. But she kept looking at Nicole, which made Nicole uneasy.

The reception was merely a matter of shaking hands with a lot of people and making small talk. The decathlon participants introduced themselves to one another and made repetitious jokes about the coming events. The officials went around congratulating the contestants and wishing them well.

Nicole would have enjoyed it, considering her newfound ability to talk to people, except that she saw a couple of police officers on the fringes of the crowd. Were they looking for the dress? Or more likely, the pearls, since they were probably very valuable. She wished she hadn't worn them. The dress didn't actually need any further decoration. She'd made a mistake.

She managed to stay on the other side of the room from the police, although she half expected to feel a tap on the shoulder at any moment.

Then the band was set up and the dance began. Bryan asked Nicole to dance right away, then a boy from another school asked her. The dress swayed and turned and dipped with each step Nicole took. It was a little difficult dancing with high heels, but Nicole managed not to step on anyone's toes. Other boys cut in, and then suddenly there was Mr. Waring standing in front of her, asking her to dance.

She drifted into his arms, and just as if it were planned, the band played a slow tune, a dreamy, dance-close-and-talk type tune. It was easier to slow-dance in the wobbly shoes.

"I guess a teacher can dance with his star pupil," Mr. Waring said in her ear. "If you feel uncomfortable about it, we can talk about the Teapot Dome scandal or the causes of the War of 1812." He grinned down at her, teasing again.

Feel uncomfortable? She'd never felt more at ease in all her life. This was where she belonged, in the arms of her beloved Mr. Waring. Her Steve. She wished he'd hold her closer. He was barely touching her.

"Let's talk about the constellations," she said. "That's what I'm seeing right now."

His grin widened, and he glanced over at Bryan, who stood on the sidelines. "Big night, eh?" he said.

He'd never understand how big. She wondered how he couldn't know, as she did, that this was the beginning of their life together. School would be out soon; that would end the teacher-student track they were stuck in right now, which of course would never allow dating. Or at least Mr. Waring's strong code of ethics would never allow it. But after graduation, they'd be free to date. Nicole could help him get over the terrible pain of losing his wife and child, and they could be married. She wondered if he'd mind if she went on to college after their marriage. Very likely he'd insist on it. Maybe he'd go back for more graduate work. Maybe they'd both go to college.

Nicole was thinking happily of a wedding gown very much like the dress she was wearing. Maybe she'd keep that very dress for her wedding. Then out of the corner of her eye she saw Tanya pointing at her. She was talking to a strange man and pointing at Nicole.

Nicole stiffened. What was Tanya saying? Was he an undercover police officer? Was she telling him that Nicole was wearing a stolen dress? Had she discovered the blue bag after Nicole left the dorm room and was she now telling him about it?

Nicole didn't dare look directly at them, but she knew the man was threading his way through the crowd. He was coming toward her!

She couldn't have him arresting her right there in front of Mr. Waring. She couldn't have him arresting her at all! How would that reflect on Tullidge High?

"Is something wrong, Nicole?" Mr. Waring was looking down at her with concern.

"Oh." What could she tell him? "Oh, it's my dress. I think I felt a seam split."

"Do you want to go check it?"Mr. Waring said.

"Yes. I'll probably have to change." She wanted to get out of the dress. Suddenly she hated it. It felt alien to her. She didn't belong in it.

She started to run across the floor, unsteady now on her high heels. All she could feel was panic. She thought of kicking off the shoes, but that would look strange and call attention to herself. Just walk casually, she told herself, but she continued to run. Was the detective following her?

"Nicole, wait." That was Tanya's voice.

She was passing the pedestal with the bust of Einstein. Just a few more yards and she'd be at the elevators. No she'd better got up the stairs. She might have to wait at the elevators.

When she felt a hand on her arm, she twisted loose, which threw her off her already precarious balance. She put her arms around the tall pedestal to steady herself, but found to her alarm that it wasn't as solid as it looked. It swayed as her weight hit it, and the bust of Einstein on top teetered. She saw it tip, then come down, the cold eyes staring at her as she struggled to get out of its way. But her ankle twisted when she tried to step aside, and she clutched at the pedestal even harder.

She felt pain, sharp, hard pain, on her head. There was confusion and moments of blackness. She was on the floor. The Einstein bust was shattered beside her. Vaguely she heard someone saying, "Don't move her! That statue could have fractured her skull. The ambulance is on the way."

Another voice, a weepy, scared-sounding female voice, said, "I don't know how it happened. I just *touched* her arm. This man was looking for her. He has a telegram for her from her parents. They probably just wanted to encourage her."

A third voice kept repeating, "Nicole! Nicole! Nicole!"

Why didn't Nicole answer?

Who *was* Nicole?

Chapter 12

Felicia was worried.

Thinking back over the events of the previous evening, she could see where holes might show up in her story about the intruder at Dean Goudy's house. For one thing, somebody had probably found the blue zippered bag where she'd left it on the bus. They might very well turn it in to the police, who would probably check it for fingerprints. What would they do when they found only hers on it?

She could say the intruder wore gloves.

Or maybe the bus driver's memory would improve and he'd tell the police that she'd got on alone.

Had she told them that the intruder had got on the bus with her?

She couldn't remember.

Her head ached, and she was due at the hospital for the early Sunday shift, the one she'd traded her Saturday shift for.

She hadn't slept well.

She wished she could call in sick. Hadn't last

night's experience been enough to warrant a day off? But somebody might ask questions about it. She wasn't sure she could recall all the details of the story she'd fabricated. She didn't want to take a chance of saying something different.

It wasn't until she was almost at the hospital that she remembered she'd have to face Robin.

But perhaps Robin hadn't discovered yet that the dress was missing. And what was there to point to her, Felicia, as the one who'd taken it anyway? So what was the big deal?

Robin was asleep when Felicia arrived to take over from the night nurse, Betty Sant.

"She's had a rough night," Betty told her as they reviewed Robin's chart at the nurses' station.

She's not the only one, Felicia thought. But all she said was, "Pain?"

"Yes, but mostly she was upset about her dress. You know, that gorgeous dress she was wearing when she was injured?" Betty's voice went up in a question, then she said, "It was stolen."

"Stolen?" Felicia put on what she hoped was a surprised look.

Betty nodded. "But it's back now, although she doesn't know it yet."

"Back?" This time Felicia didn't have to pretend to be surprised.

Betty nodded again. "Funniest thing. It came in on a girl with a head injury last night. The nurse who admitted her recognized the dress. Well, I mean, who could forget it once they'd seen it? Anyway, it's back in Robin's closet now, along with the shoes. We're going to insist that she send them home with her family today. We don't know what to do about the pearls, though."

Felicia was sure she heard the click of a trap closing around her. The girl who'd been brought in wearing the dress must have been on the bus and could very well have seen her with the blue bag. She might be able to identify her, and she'd be arrested for stealing the pearls from the Goudys, and then charged, too, with stealing the dress. Mark would never want to see her again.

"Excuse me," she said. She was going to say she was sick, that she had to go home. She had to get out of there before the girl who'd had the dress on could see her and maybe recognize her.

"That poor girl can't tell us anything." Betty was still speaking. "Her head injury has caused total amnesia."

Felicia's heart slowed as she imagined the big steel trap slowly separating again. Amnesia! Then even if she'd seen Felicia, she wouldn't remember.

Robin didn't awaken until Felicia brought her breakfast tray.

"Well, hello," Felicia said, "how are you this nice morning?" It was a much nicer morning than it had started out to be, that was for sure. She was safe, at least for now. But how long could that last? There were too many things for her to keep control of. Something she hadn't even thought of could start to unravel the whole story.

But right now her responsibility was to her patient. At least she could make sure she didn't mess up there.

Robin was frowning, as if trying to remember something. Then her face drooped. "My dress," she said. "It's gone."

"Your dress?" Felicia said brightly. "Why, it's right here." Putting down the breakfast tray, she flung open the closet door to show Robin, who blinked in astonishment.

"But it was gone last night."

Felicia almost said that she must have dreamed that it was gone. Robin would believe that, since she still had moments of fogginess from pain medication. But then she remembered that other people knew it had been gone. She had to be careful what she said.

Looking at the dress, she felt a little sick to her stomach, remembering the way it had almost choked off her breath.

She closed the closet door.

"I'll tell you what I know about it while I get you cleaned up for breakfast," she said. "We'd better hurry, or your eggs will be cold."

She didn't tell Robin *everything* she knew. Just the part about the girl who came in wearing it.

"But how did she get it?" Robin asked when Felicia had finished the story. "Did she come in here and take it while I was asleep?"

Felicia was glad Robin had said it. She didn't want to suggest it herself. She didn't want any more lies on her soul. She merely didn't deny it.

"Don't worry about it anymore, Robin. We'll be sending the dress home with your mother and sister if they come today." She didn't mention the pearls. She'd let somebody else ask Robin about them. She didn't want to be connected with them in any way.

"No," Robin said. "No."

She was quite emphatic. "I don't want to send the dress home."

"It would be safer there," Felicia said. Besides, if the dress was out of sight, people might stop wondering how the girl with the head injury had come to have it in the first place.

"No," Robin said again. She seemed to think for a moment, then asked, "Was that girl injured as bad as I am?"

Felicia felt something cold creep through her body. Robin's soft question made her think of something that hadn't occurred to her before. Each girl who'd worn the dress recently had been injured somehow. Robin and the other girl had been physically hurt. She, Felicia, had been morally impaired. Her integrity had been ruined, in her own eyes, at least. She'd never lied before, except for the little white kind that people say to make other people feel better. She was lucky that it hadn't been any worse. But the cold feeling kept spreading. Robin had wanted to be a dancer, and her feet were smashed. She, Felicia, had wanted to be pure and spotless in Mark's eyes, and now she knew she wasn't. Would he know soon? Was there some clue she'd forgotten to cover up?

Was she going to have to tell Mark?

No. No. She couldn't even think of that. She'd already lost too much.

What had the third girl lost through her injury? Was there a pattern? Was the dress going to cause them all further injury?

Panic swept her out of Robin's room and down the hall where the other girl lay, her head swathed in bandages. The girl stared blankly at her as she burst through the door. There was a boy sitting on a chair beside her bed.

Felicia took a deep breath. "Hi. I'm just checking to see how you're doing." The girl wouldn't know she wasn't her assigned nurse.

"I'm okay, I guess," the girl said.

"How does your head feel?"

"It hurts."

Briskly Felicia walked over and put her fingers on the girl's pulse, trying to look official, and at the same time eyeing her hospital bracelet to see what her name was. Nicole Eckhart. "Have you had any medication this morning, Nicole?"

The girl looked blank.

"She doesn't know her name," the boy said softly. "She's lost her memory." He introduced himself. "I'm Bryan Bentley."

"It happened last night, I understand. I'm sorry."

The boy nodded, looking glum. "We were at a reception for all the academic decathlon participants."

Felicia figured that questions must have appeared on her face because the guy explained, "The academic decathlon is a contest about how much you know. We're competing with teams from other high schools. Nicole is the star of our team. She's about the smartest person I know."

So this girl *had* lost something, too. The dress had taken away her memory. Her knowledge. Nicole Eckhart was the third girl to lose something while she was wearing the dress.

"She's also about the prettiest," the boy continued. He took Nicole's hand. "You should have seen her last night. She was the most beautiful girl in the room."

"Was I?" Nicole's eyes were empty.

"I have to go," Felicia said, as she felt the room become colder.

"Wait a minute," Bryan said. "I'll walk out with you. I have to get back to the decathlon anyway. I don't know what we'll do without Nicole." He squeezed Nicole's hand and kissed her on the forehead.

A nice guy, Felicia thought. Like Mark, who was surely lost to her.

"Don't worry," Bryan said to Nicole. "Your folks will be here soon. And the rest of the team and I will be back later to tell you how we did."

The girl gave him an uncomprehending smile. She picked up the edge of the sheet that covered her and gazed at it, her eyes unfocused. She pulled it up to hold against her cheek. "Nice," she said.

The guy looked as if his heart would break. "Oh, Nicole," he whispered, then turned to go. Felicia followed him.

Outside the door of the room, he asked, "Do you think she's going to be all right?"

"You'd better talk to her doctor," Felicia said. "I'm just a nurse." But the boy looked so miserable that she added, "A lot of amnesia victims get their memories back eventually."

"Eventually." Bryan nodded glumly. "I wish it could be right now. Not only because of the decathlon, but because they want to question her about how she got the dress and pearls she was wearing last night. Somebody said they were stolen. I sure don't want her to get in trouble."

In trouble for something she, Felicia, did. But then Nicole wasn't innocent, either. She'd taken the dress, too. She must have found it on the bus.

"I have to go," Felicia said again.

"Thanks for your concern." Bryan put out his hand.

Felicia laid a limp hand in his, then hurried back to Robin's room.

Robin was sitting up, poking at her cold breakfast.

Felicia went over to the bed and sank into the chair next to it. She looked at Robin's pale face for a moment and then said slowly, "The dress, Robin, there is something wrong with the dress. Something evil. I know it."

Robin looked at Felicia in silence. Then she said softly, "Go on."

"Every girl who has worn that dress in the last weeks has had something terrible happen to her. Every girl has lost something important to her while she was wearing that dress. . . ."

Robin continued looking at Felicia, waiting.

Felicia stood up and walked to the window and

stared out. Then she turned back to Robin. "You are a dancer, and your feet were mangled. Nicole, the girl with the head injury, she was a brilliant student, and it took away her memory. And I . . . it took away my. . . ."

Felicia hadn't meant to confess her part in the whole thing. She had just wanted to make sure no other girl wore that dress. That dress that looked so beautiful and innocent and was so fiercesome and ugly.

But it was too late to stop now.

"It took away my integrity." She realized just how much she'd lost when she thought about how she'd been willing to let Nicole take the blame for taking the dress from Robin's room.

She looked steadily at Robin. "I took the dress, Robin. I took it from the closet while you were sleeping Friday night."

Robin nodded. "I know."

"You knew?"

"While you were gone I remembered that it was you who was dancing with the dress after you showed it to me one night. Remember? I was worried about the dress and wanted to see it. I didn't see you take it, but I knew how much you liked it."

Felicia was suddenly glad she'd confessed before she'd been accused. "I took it the next night. I needed it for a party. I don't usually do things like that. But the dress seemed to get into my mind and I couldn't get it out. I was obsessed by it. I had to have it."

Robin nodded again. "It happened that way with me, too."

Felicia wasn't surprised. "I wish we could ask Nicole how it affected her."

"I think we know," Robin said. She shivered and pushed away the table that held her breakfast tray. "Felicia, what did it do to you? You said it took away your integrity. What happened?"

She patted the edge of her bed, indicating that Felicia should sit down. Instead, Felica drew the chair close to the bed and sat down. "I shouldn't take the time. I have other patients. . . ." She stopped and cleared her throat. "This is what happened, Robin."

She told her story quickly, leaving nothing out. She watched sympathy soften Robin's pain-pinched face. When she was finished, she stood up, and Robin reached for her hand, holding it without saying anything.

"Robin," Felicia said. "We have to destroy that dress."

Robin's grasp on her hand tightened. "No! We can't do that!" She looked frightened, almost terrified.

"Why not?" Felicia asked. "It seems like the only thing to do."

Tears suddenly ran down Robin's face. "It's Miss Catherine, the woman I took it from. I don't know what it is . . . but she frightens me. I feel she would do something awful to me if she knew I had taken her dress. I have to get the dress back to her attic closet, so she never knows I ever had it."

Felicia didn't want to upset Robin any more than she already was. "Can't we send it home with your mother and sister? We have to get it out of here before some other girl takes it, wears it, and. . . ."

"I don't want Gabby near that dress," Robin said. "I can't let her see it."

Felicia thought for a moment. "Couldn't we wrap it in something? Then Gabby wouldn't even know what it was."

Mopping at her tears with a tissue, Robin gazed out of the window, and then said, "I could have Gabby bring the garment bag I used when. . . ." She paused and then went on firmly, "when I took the dress from Miss Catherine's closet. If I tell Gabby *not* to open the bag, to just put it in my closet, she'll do that. She's a good kid."

"Robin, you have to tell Gabby what the danger is," Felicia warned. "You have to tell her about you and me and Nicole."

"No," Robin shouted. "I don't want anyone to know I *took* the dress."

"Think about it," Felicia said. "You're asking her to take an awful risk. She should know the whole story, just so she'll be prepared."

Robin's eyes were full of misery. "No. The less she knows, the better. She'd just say it was a coincidence that awful things happened when we wore the dress. She'd want to test it out. If I ask her not to open the bag, she won't."

"I hope not," Felicia said.

Gabby was there in Robin's room when Felicia came back after her lunch break. Her sister and the boy named Tyler who'd been Robin's prom date. They must have come together. Gabby was laughing and talking with animation, and every now and then her eyes would slide over to Tyler. Her shining face told Felicia that Gabby felt more than mere friendship for Tyler.

From Robin's bleak look, Felicia guessed that Robin saw it, too.

But Felicia couldn't worry about that. She had problems of her own, some confessions she had to make. Otherwise that poor girl Nicole was going to be in big trouble for having the dress and Mrs. Goudy's pearls in her possession. There'd been a policeman at the nurses' station when she'd passed. Had he been asking questions about Nicole?

She was going to call Mark and have him meet her. She was going to tell him that everything she'd said the night before had been a lie. Then she was going to go to the police.

It was the only way she could hope to save any shred of her decency.

Chapter 13

Tyler was with Robin when Gabrielle arrived at the hospital with the garment bag Robin had asked her to bring. She was glad to see him. He hadn't been at the house since Robin's accident. Gabrielle had missed him. A lot. She'd planned her visit to Robin for a time when she thought he'd be there. And if things worked out — well, maybe he'd come around more.

Robin barely greeted her before she had the nurse take the garment bag and stuff the prom dress inside. Gabrielle was a little puzzled by Robin's strict instructions about taking the dress home.

"Go right home," Robin said. "Hang it *right in my closet* when you get there. And Gabby, *don't* take it out of the bag. Don't even open it. Just take it upstairs and *leave it alone.*" Her voice was getting high and shrill.

What was Robin hysterical about? What did she think Gabby would do? Take the dress out and play house with it the way she did once with Robin's best clothes when she was a little kid?

"Yes, Sergeant." Gabrielle clicked her heels and saluted. Usually that made Robin laugh, but today she was serious and nervous. "Why don't I just run it back over to Miss Catherine for you? Then you won't have to worry about it."

"No!"

Even Tyler looked surprised by Robin's sharpness.

Robin exchanged an odd glance with the nurse, then took a deep breath. "No," Robin repeated, calmer now. "Do what I say, Gabby. Just put it in my closet, okay?"

"Okay," Gabby agreed. She watched the glowing dress disappear as the nurse zipped up the bag. It was a shame to imprison all that beauty. "I guess it's safer in the bag. I wouldn't want to have the dress brushing against the dirty floor of the bus on the way home."

Tyler was watching her. "I'll carry it," he said, taking the dark garment bag from the nurse. "I'll give it a lift home, just to make sure it arrives safely."

"What about me?" Gabby protested. "Doesn't anybody care if *I* get home safely?"

Tyler grinned. "Sure, kid. I guess I can find room for you, too."

Gabrielle could barely restrain herself from giving a little skip of joy. Tyler had made things so easy. And now that the ride home was arranged, it was just one more short step to invite him to stay and play piano duets with her. She'd been so lonely without either Robin or Tyler around.

Robin was looking troubled. She glanced from

Tyler to Gabrielle, then back to Tyler. "The dress will be safe enough on the bus," she said.

Gabrielle held her breath. Had Robin guessed how she felt about Tyler? Had her face given something away, her little kid's face that tattled all her emotions?

She didn't want to hurt Robin. Truly. But Robin went through guys the way some girls went through toothpaste, casting them aside when she was tired of them. Well, it wasn't *quite* that way. But she'd had several boyfriends who'd come around for a while and then were gone, even back in Newton. Gabrielle had never had anybody, and especially somebody like Tyler, who loved the piano as much as she did.

Gabrielle didn't intend to take him away from Robin, or anything like that. She just wanted to make sure he knew she was there when the time came that Robin was through with him. After all, he wasn't so much older than she was.

"Give the kid a break," Tyler said. "My car's a little nicer than the bus." He leaned over to give Robin a kiss. "I'll be by to spring you from this place as soon as the doctor gives you a pardon."

Robin did smile at that. "It should be in a few days. Gabby, *be sure* to take that dress right upstairs as *soon* as you get home."

Gabrielle nodded, and Tyler draped the garment bag over his shoulder, hooking the dress hanger over one finger. Then he motioned to Gabrielle.

"Come on, kid. Let's get Operation Dress To Closet under way."

They left Robin's hospital room together. Gabrielle wished he wouldn't keep calling her "kid." After all, she was almost fifteen. Well, in ten months she'd be fifteen.

On the other hand, the fact that he did call her that ought to put Robin's mind at rest.

As soon as they were far enough away so that Robin wouldn't see, Gabrielle took Tyler's free hand, swinging it a bit so that is would seem like a little-girl gesture.

"Tyler. Guess what?" She looked up at him through the fringe of her eyelashes, the way she'd been practicing, although not with him specifically in mind. For a while she'd thought any boy would do, just someone to go out with. But that was before Tyler started sitting on the piano bench beside her, playing duets from the book her teacher had given her.

Now he grinned at her, kind of a big-brother to-kid-sister grin. Gabrielle was satisfied with that.

"I can't guess," he said.

"I've been practicing the 'Poet and Peasant Overture' like mad," she said. "That one we played the last time you were at my house."

His eyes darkened a little. He was probably remembering that that had been prom night, the night Robin was injured. But then he grinned again and said, "It didn't seem to me you needed much practice. You were sight-reading just fine."

"I wanted to get it perfect for the next time we play together." Gabrielle gave a little-girl skip. "How about staying for a while today, as long as you're dropping me off anyway?" When

Tyler glanced back at Robin's room, she went on quickly. "I was thinking we'd get that duet all worked up as a coming-home present for Robin. Something fun to surprise her with."

"Well, okay," Tyler said. "I didn't have anything else planned for the afternoon."

Gabrielle pretended to pout. "That's really flattering. You mean since you can't think of anything else to do, you'll let yourself be coaxed into spending a boring afternoon with me."

He grinned. "That isn't what I said." Letting go of her hand, he put his arm around her as they went along the hallway. Inside the garment bag, Robin's dress slipped around, whispering an accompaniment as they walked. It seemed to be almost speaking to Gabby. No, not Robin's dress. It was Miss Catherine's. Gabrielle was glad Robin had told her not to take it back yet, because she was sure that the dress was whispering, "Look at me, Gabby. Look at me."

She might just do that, up in Robin's room, before she buried it away in the dark closet. She remembered its creamy beauty and the way she'd loved it the first moment she'd seen it. It was more her kind of dress than Robin's, anyway, although it wasn't the ragbag kind of stuff she usually wore. She'd unzip the bag in Robin's room and just look at the dress. Nothing could happen to it there, and just looking at it couldn't make it dirty, or tear it, or anything. What was Robin so worried about anyway?

"Hey, kid," Tyler said, "need to rewind your tape?"

They were at his car now, and he was opening the passenger door for her.

"Tape?" Gabrielle was puzzled.

"You've been so quiet for the past few minutes I thought maybe you'd come to the end of your tape."

She laughed. "Just the moment of silence before the next number begins." She got into the car, and he handed the garment bag to her. The dress inside whispered again as she laid it across her lap. *Look at me. Look at me.*

When he slid into the driver's seat, she said, "If it's chatter you want, I'll provide it if you'll show me how fast this clunker can go."

"Clunker!" he yowled. "Hey, woman, are you in for a surprise!"

They both laughed as he started the car, then burned off a layer of rubber before they even got out of the parking lot.

"You're a lot different from Robin," he said, sending her an appreciative glance.

Tyler stayed at Gabrielle's house for hours. They sat close together on the piano bench, playing one duet after another. They practiced the "Poet and Peasant Overture" until they could play it without a single sour note. They did "Marche Militaire" and the "Turkish March," which left them flushed and warm. Just for fun they did "Norwegian Dance" and "Country Gardens." Last, they played Schumann's haunting "Traumerei," and when the last poignant note died away Gabrielle thought for sure Tyler was going to kiss her. He turned and looked at her, his face just inches from hers. For a long moment Gabrielle felt like one of the girls from the romance novels Robin read, all trembly with anticipation.

"That was nice, Gabrielle," he said, then stood up to go.

At least he hadn't called her "kid."

Gabrielle was still thinking about Tyler when she took the garment bag to Robin's room. She'd left it draped over a chair in the living room while Tyler was there. Now it was time to carry it upstairs where she could peek at it.

The dress rustled excitedly inside the bag, and Garielle's heart thumped. She knew why now. Actually, she'd known it before, at the hospital, but she hadn't let herself admit it. She was going to do more than just look at the dress. She was going to wear it. For Tyler.

She didn't know how or where. But that would all work out. It would have to be soon, since Robin would be coming home in a few days, and it had to be before that. Or maybe it didn't. Robin wouldn't be returning the dress the very instant she came home. There was time.

In Robin's yellow-wallpapered room Gabby unzipped the garment bag, and the dress almost leapt out of its dark prison. It was even more beautiful than Gabrielle had remembered, with its old-fashioned lace and flounces. When she wore it, she'd do her hair up in a thick French braid. She'd put on ivory stockings and the spool-heeled shoes she'd bought at an attic sale. She'd give the impression of youth and innocence. A kid. But the dress would bring out everything in her that was neither young nor innocent. She held the dress up against her and swayed in front of Robin's full-length mirror, gazing dreamily at herself through half-closed eyes. For a moment she thought she saw a smudge on her left cheek, but when she opened her eyes wide, it was gone. All she saw was a pretty girl and a beautiful dress.

Tyler would like her better than Robin.

Realizing what she was thinking, Gabrielle was shocked. She threw the dress down on the bed. How could she even think things like that? The thoughts just seemed to creep into her mind as she looked at the dress. She snatched up the garment bag, intending to put the dress back inside. She couldn't wear it, and she couldn't stand there coldly plotting to take over her own sister's boyfriend. She'd just have to wait around until Robin went on to the next boy. By then she herself would have grown out of the "kid" stage.

The dress rustled softly as she picked it up. She looked at it for a moment, then walked back to the mirror again, holding it up against herself. It clung to her, begging to be worn. Its color was so perfect for her. It brightened her brown hair and made her blue eyes look soft and . . . what? Alluring, maybe?

She smiled at herself in the mirror and was amazed at how much older she looked already.

Chapter 14

It was four days later that Robin's doctor told her she could go home the next day.

"You'll have to come in every week as an outpatient," he told her. "But you'd probably rather be home until the next surgery on your feet."

That was the truth. Robin appreciated all they'd done for her at the hospital, but she didn't care to hang around any longer than necessary. Besides, she had to get home, where she could see that the prom dress was put securely back into Miss Catherine's attic closet. It wasn't something she could shove off on somebody else. She'd have to get Gabby to take it up all those stairs, of course, since she couldn't do it herself. But the most important thing was to get the dress hidden away again. . . . Then Miss Catherine would never know Robin had taken it, and no other girl would find it.

Felicia agreed.

"I still think we should destroy the dress," Felicia said when she was helping Robin get ready to go home. "We should burn it or something."

Robin shivered, even though the room was warm. "I don't know what would happen if we tried that." She'd had a nightmare about burning the dress. It had risen from the flames like the legendary phoenix bird, which rose from its own ashes. It had come toward her through the smoky air, and as it came closer, she'd seen that someone was wearing it, someone with a huge, dark splotch on the left side of her face.

No, she wasn't going to try to destroy the dress. It might not be possible, and that terrified her.

Her throat felt tight, and she cleared it before going on. "It's not ours to destroy, anyway. As I said before, we don't know for sure that the things that happened wouldn't have occurred regardless of what we were wearing."

Felicia was clearing up some flower petals that had dried up and dropped off an arrangement Tyler had sent. She paused, looking steadily at Robin. "You don't believe that, do you?"

Robin shifted nervously. "I'm just trying to make sense of the whole thing."

"Well, try making sense of having a dress try to choke you to death, the way that — that *thing* did on the night of Dean Goudy's dinner party."

"You were feeling guilty," Robin said. "Maybe your conscience was bothering you so much that you imagined the dress was squeezing you."

Felicia gave her a look that made Robin put her hands up as if to shield herself.

"Okay, okay. I know there's something evil about that dress," Robin said. "But it's safe in my closet now. I *have* to return it to its owner."

Felicia busied herself with the flowers again. "You have to tell her what happened."

Robin groaned, "I can't." Thinking about that, she flushed. It wasn't Miss Catherine's fault the dress had been worn. She'd warned Robin that the dress couldn't leave the house. "The dress will never leave the attic again. No one goes up there."

"I hope so."

"Did you tell Mark?" Robin asked gently.

Felicia nodded silently.

Robin waited.

When Felicia turned to face her, Robin saw that tears were streaming down her cheeks.

"Felicia." She reached out a hand to touch Felicia's. "I'm sorry."

"You can't even imagine how awful it was." Felicia scrubbed fiercely at her eyes with her free hand. "He didn't say much, but I could feel his total disappointment in me. It was my character that he admired about me, and I totally wiped it out. He thought I was direct and up front and good. I told him the whole truth, and I haven't heard from him since. He said he'd call, but he hasn't yet." She paused. "Robin, would you believe the *truth* about the dress? It sounded more phony than all the lies I'd made up. Now he doesn't know what to believe. And the police and the Goudys — I'm sure they think I'm just trying to cover the theft of the pearls with another wild story. I'm not right for a minister's wife."

"Are they pressing charges?" Robin asked softly.

Felicia drooped. "I don't know. They're very upset."

Robin squeezed the nurse's limp hand.

"I can't even imagine how I could have done what I did. But that dress, that beautiful, *terrible* dress — it almost seemed to reach out to me when it was hanging in the closet. I couldn't seem to escape it."

Robin nodded. She knew the feeling. "It seems to have some kind of power." She tried to block out a foreboding she'd had ever since she'd sent the dress home with Gabby, a feeling that the dress might reach out through its dark shroud and draw Gabby into its power.

"I told Gabby not even to *open* the bag," she said. "She told me again yesterday that it's shut safely away in my closet."

There was another thing Robin didn't want to think about, and that was the way Gabby and Tyler had showed up together every day since she'd sent the dress home. She knew they'd been practicing their piano duets a lot, and there was a good reason for that. They'd told her they had a gig, an actual paying job playing the piano in the background at an elegant afternoon party given by Mrs. Chandler, one of Forest Dale's richest women. Gabby's piano teacher had recommended Gabby, who in turn suggested that she and Tyler play duets. Mrs. Chandler had liked the idea.

But why did they have to come to the hospital

together? Robin and Tyler never had any time alone anymore.

Did Gabrielle plan it that way?

Shaking her head to remove such thoughts from it, Robin changed the subject. "Felicia, how is Nicole doing now?"

Felicia wiped away the last traces of her tears with one of Robin's tissues and put on her professional air again. "She went home with her parents yesterday. She's regained a little of her memory, but not enough to go back to school and who knows whether it will all come back."

"What about the young man who came to see her every day? Did she ever remember him?"

"Bryan? She had a few memories concerning him, mostly of when they were in the early grades together. But their decathlon coach came to see her one day and she was totally blank about him."

"Poor Nicole," Robin said.

Poor Felicia.

Poor Robin.

On the day Robin was released, her mother, Gabby, and Tyler all came to get her. They would have come in Tyler's little red Trans Am, except that there wasn't room for four people plus the newly purchased wheelchair.

They came to get her in the old family station wagon.

"Tyler and I have a first-class welcome for you at home," Gabby assured her.

When they got there, they drove around through the back alley so they could wheel her chair straight into the house. Both their house and Miss Catherine's house sat against a small hill so that there were no stairs to obstruct her wheelchair in the back.

Even so, it was a real downer to have to be wheeled into that house, through which she had danced so many times. Gabby and Tyler's "first-class welcome" helped a little, although Robin could hardly concentrate on it, thinking about the dress hanging upstairs and how she was going to have to take it over to Miss Catherine. She wished she could do it now and get it over with. But she couldn't leave during the little concert in her honor.

What Gabby and Tyler played was a rousing medley of Sousa marches. Robin liked marches, and they were different from the music she'd danced to. Their polished performance showed that they'd spent a lot of time practicing, sitting close together there on the piano bench.

"You're wonderful," she told them. "When is this paying job you have?"

"Saturday," Gabby said. "It's going to be terrific. I wish you could come. It's a dress-up affair, and Tyler is going to wear a tux."

"And what will you wear?" Robin held her breath, waiting for Gabby to answer.

"Oh," Gabby said casually, "remember that pink prom dress Mom's friend's daughter offered to let you wear?"

Robin almost laughed with relief. Had she really suspected Gabby would be pulled to the evil dress? Music was what was important to

Gabby. She'd probably throw some of the ragbag stuff she picked up in the thrift shops on over that pink dress and look stunning.

"I wish I could come, too," Robin said. "But you'll just have to tell me all about it when you get home. Besides, I'm not invited."

"I think Miss Catherine wants you to come over to her house that day anyway," her mother said. "She called a couple of days ago to ask if you'd feel up to it. She said she'd call again when you got home. Do you think you'll be strong enough?"

"Yes," Robin said. But she wondered if she'd ever be strong enough to face Miss Catherine, for she had decided to tell Miss Catherine the truth. She just hadn't been able to think of a way to get the dress into the attic without *someone* knowing the truth. And what could Miss Catherine do that would be so terrible?

Miss Catherine did call on Saturday, and she issued an invitation to what almost seemed like a command performance. "I want to see you, dear," she said. "Please come in the late afternoon."

It was arranged that Gabby would take Robin over and then would go off to the party with Tyler, and their mother would come over to get Robin as soon as she got home from doing Saturday errands.

Robin hoped her mother wouldn't be delayed. Miss Catherine would very likely be furious about the confession she was going to make.

Robin didn't want to be stuck there with no way to get home if Miss Catherine's fury was too much for her to handle.

When it was time to go, Gabby brought the dress, still in the garment bag, downstairs to the den, which had been made into a bedroom for Robin until she recovered.

"Do you want to check it out before we go?" Gabby asked, holding up the bag.

"No." Robin didn't want to see that dress again. Ever.

Gabby laid the bag across Robin's lap. It felt light, which somehow surprised Robin. She'd thought it would weigh as heavy as her conscience.

Gabby grasped the handles of the wheelchair and they started out through the back door. "Are you sure you'll be okay over there until Mom comes?"

She seemed excited. She was probably nervous about her piano-playing engagement that afternoon. She was already dressed in the pink dress.

"I'll be fine," Robin said.

"Okay. I won't stay to visit. Tyler will be here real soon."

Robin wished she could wait and at least greet Tyler. But she knew how Miss Catherine was about her arriving promptly. She could see him after Mrs. Chandler's party. Gabby had promised they'd play their whole program for her then.

Miss Catherine called out for them to come in when they knocked at her back door. "I left the door unlocked," she said.

Robin took a deep breath. She hoped Miss Catherine would quietly get rid of the dress so that she'd never have to tell anyone else. "Let's go in," she told Gabby. She smoothed the garment bag lying across her lap.

"I'll run the dress upstairs before I leave," Gabby said.

"No." Robin put her palms flat on the garment bag. "Miss Catherine can do it."

Gabby hesitated. "I'll save her the trouble. I'm sure she won't want to climb all those stairs."

"It's all right, Gabby," Robin said. "Maybe she'll just hang it downstairs for a while." She wished Gabby would just push her inside and leave so she could get this over with.

"Then I'll hang it in a back closet for you," Gabby insisted.

"Forget it, Gabby! Just take me inside!" Robin could hear the sharp edge in her voice.

Without another word, Gabby opened the back door and pushed the wheelchair into the hallway.

Miss Catherine was in her sunken parlor, sitting as usual in the blue-striped Morris chair. The room was dark, even though the drapes were open. Shadows hung in the corners like the cobwebs in the closet upstairs. It was so cold Robin wished she'd brought a sweater. Was it really that cold or was it just that Robin was remembering how everything had started here in this house?

Gabby helped Robin out of her wheelchair while she eased it down the three steps to the parlor, then helped her get back in it, with the garment bag on her lap.

"Oh, my dear," Miss Catherine said, holding out her hands but not rising. "How I've missed you." She motioned for Gabby to push Robin close enough so she could give her a soft peck on the cheek.

"I hope your trip was pleasant," Robin said.

"As pleasant as it could be, under the circumstances." Miss Catherine waved a hand toward the sofa. "Sit down, Gabrielle. I'd like to visit with you, too."

Gabby made her excuses, told Miss Catherine that their mother would come to get Robin, and left, hurrying across the soft carpeting to the back door. She could have stayed a few minutes. Did she have to be *that* eager to go over to wait for Tyler?

"Now tell me about your *dreadful* accident," Miss Catherine said to Robin. "I've only heard Gabrielle's version." She didn't even ask about the garment bag on Robin's lap.

Reluctantly Robin sketched out what had happened. Miss Catherine wanted to know all the details of the accident. "The throne fell right on your feet, you say? Tell me what that felt like."

Robin didn't want to relive the horror of that moment, but she told Miss Catherine what she could. Miss Catherine had an odd reaction to the story. She became excited, almost agitated. The scarred side of her face twitched.

"And the dress," she said. "Did it ruin the dress?"

Did Miss Catherine know about the dress? How could she?

"You thought I didn't know, but of course I

did. Right from the start." Miss Catherine smiled, a strange, cold smile.

Robin swallowed hard. "The dress is fine, Miss Catherine. I have it right here in this bag." She took a deep breath, preparing to tell her the whole story.

Miss Catherine nodded. "It was fine the last time, too."

"The last time?" Robin said.

But Miss Catherine wasn't looking at Robin. She was gazing past her, out of the window, over at Robin's house.

Gabby had positioned Robin's wheelchair so that her back was to that window. Now Robin wheeled the chair around so she could see what Miss Catherine was watching with a twisted, gleeful smile.

Over at her own house Robin saw Tyler on the porch. Gabby came out and, stretching up on tiptoe, kissed him on the cheek.

Gabby was wearing the prom dress. Its creamy beauty contrasted elegantly with her dark hair. She looked slender and fragile and terribly appealing with the deep scallops of lace draping sweetly over her hips.

Robin could almost hear the dress rustle as Gabby moved. "Oh, no!" she whispered.

Miss Catherine chuckled, deep in her throat. "It's happening again. Just like Catherine and Michael. Sister against sister." Her chuckle became a giggle.

Robin felt ill. Her heart raced so that it was like a fast drumbeat in her ears, and she felt as if she were going to be sick.

Gabby hadn't put the prom dress in the garment bag at all. She was wearing it for Tyler. She'd planned all this. She'd probably planned it since the day she'd taken the dress home.

Something stirred inside Robin. It was like a seed that had lain dormant for a long time but now had suddenly sprouted an ugly, malignant growth.

Hate. That's what it was. It was an unfamiliar emotion for Robin. She hated Gabby for plotting behind her back while she was injured. Gabby was in love with Tyler, probably had been ever since that first time she'd so innocently invited him to sit on the piano bench with her. She was no kid. She was a calculating, conniving woman. And she was taking Robin's boyfriend, just the way Catherine had taken Rowena's young man.

She wondered how she knew that. Miss Catherine hadn't told her.

"She thought I didn't know," Miss Catherine muttered. "But I knew, even before the prom." She put her hand up to gently stroke the twitching scar. "Catherine always took everything she wanted. She was so beautiful."

What was she talking about? *She* was Catherine.

"I don't understand," Robin said, wheeling closer to Miss Catherine.

Miss Catherine looked at her with unfocused eyes that reminded Robin of Nicole's, but hers were not empty. They smoldered with what Robin recognized as hate. Hate, like Robin felt for Gabrielle.

"Catherine took Michael from me," she said hoarsely. "She had all those others to choose from. But she wanted Michael, too."

"But," Robin protested, *"you're* Catherine."

Miss Catherine smiled. This time it was a sly, secretive smile.

The realization hit Robin with a suddenness that made her gasp. This wasn't Miss Catherine at all. *This* was Rowena.

"Rowena?" she said aloud.

"Yes, of course. Rowena. *I'm* Rowena." She nodded as if to herself. "And now it's happening all over again." She looked over at Gabby and Tyler.

Robin wanted to roll her wheelchair out of there, out of the back door, out into the fresh air, away from Rowena. But she couldn't get out alone. She needed help. She could never get it up those three steps to the main level of the house. So she sat as if mesmerized, watching her own house. Gabby was beckoning to Tyler to come inside, making gestures that must mean she'd forgotten something.

Tyler went in.

The malignant thing inside Robin writhed and grew larger. "She's wearing the prom dress," she whispered.

"Oh, yes, yes, yes!" Miss Catherine — not Miss Catherine, but Rowena — rose from her chair and clapped her hands. "Yes, she's wearing the prom dress." She turned to Robin. "I cursed every stitch of that dress. I started it for myself, you know. I thought Michael was going to ask me to the prom. But I had the birthmark, you see, and Catherine was the beauty. That was the most important thing in the world to her, as Michael was to me. I saw them sneak around together, and when he asked her to the prom I finished the dress for her, because I knew it was the last time she would ever be beautiful."

Rowena jiggled up and down. "When they came home, I threw acid on her face. But not on the dress. I didn't want to ruin the dress. She was wearing a cloak, so it didn't get on the dress. I didn't want to hurt the dress. I did it right there in the foyer, on our little stage." Rowena gave a mirthless laugh. "After that she was even uglier than I was."

Catherine had lost her beauty, and Robin had lost her dancing feet. And Felicia! Nicole! Oh, the malice of that hideous dress! It took away what was most important to those who wore it, the thing whose absence would make their lives empty and barren. That was the unfailing pattern it followed.

And Gabby?

Robin watched the house next door with narrowed eyes. Tyler and Gabby came out on the porch, and Gabby swayed her hips as she walked beside Tyler.

Gabby in the cursed dress.

Gabby, who would lose something, too. What was most important to Gabby? Her long-fingered, piano-playing hands. That's what it would be, of course.

"Let her go," Rowena said. "She deserves it."

Yes. Let her go.

Robin turned her chair around again so she wouldn't have to watch Tyler open the passenger door of the red Trans Am for Gabrielle to get in.

Let her go!

Chapter 15

Robin wondered later what would have happened if she hadn't turned her head for one last look. What she saw was Gabby looking toward Miss Catherine's house. Rowena's house.

Gabby's little fourteen-year-old child's face was troubled and guilty-looking.

It almost seemed as if Gabby were reaching out to her.

Robin felt the hatred drain out of her. She wished she could turn the clock back to the moment when she herself was conscience-stricken about taking the dress. She wished there'd been someone to give her strength so that she could have overpowered the dress and reversed her decision.

"Gabby," she screamed. "Stop!"

Rowena laughed wildly. "Let her go, let her go," she chanted. "Let the dress take care of her. It knows the proper punishment."

Robin wheeled her chair around and headed

for the front door. But there were steps, three impossible barriers.

"Rowena," she screamed, "help me!"

But Rowena was crooning to herself as she watched through the window. Robin doubted if she even heard. She'd retreated into some maniacal world of her own.

"Gabby!" Robin screamed again. She hadn't heard the car door slam yet. Tyler was probably helping Gabby to get all of the lacy edges of the dress safely inside before he shut the door, the way he'd done when Robin wore it. There was time.

Painfully Robin pushed herself to a standing position. Those great iron teeth she remembered so well gnashed at her feet, and the heavy casts clunked against the first step.

She felt faint.

"Don't let go yet," she instructed herself firmly.

She couldn't take a step up, so she fell against the stairs, heaving herself to the foyer level. Then, inch by painful inch, she pulled herself across the polished floor and wrestled the door open.

Rowena came to stand behind her. "I knew you took it," she said. "Once I planted the idea of the forbidden dress in your mind, I knew you'd search it out. And once you saw it, you'd take it. The more you resisted, the stronger it became, until you *had* to have it. Catherine couldn't resist it, either, even though she knew I had meant it for myself. She couldn't resist it any more than she could resist enticing Michael."

"But why did you want to punish *me*?" Robin cried out. "I wasn't taking Tyler away from anybody."

"Oh, but you're young and beautiful." Rowena spoke as if Robin ought to understand that. Her voice lowered. "I hate *all* beautiful young girls who have no trouble attracting beaux."

At that moment Robin heard the door of Tyler's car slam. Now Tyler would be walking around to his side of the car. He'd get in. He'd start the car and they'd be gone. And Gabby's beautiful talented hands would be ruined. Maybe Tyler would drive too fast. Maybe there'd be a crash.

Robin was still more than five feet away from the door. Somehow she had to get there. That was Gabby out there. Her *sister*. She wasn't like Rowena. She wouldn't hurt her sister. No, not even if Gabby took Tyler away from her. She couldn't send her out, knowing what Rowena's malevolent dress would do to her.

Clenching her jaw against the pain, Robin grasped the back of a chair in the foyer and again pulled herself up so that she was standing on her broken feet enclosed in the heavy casts. Sweating with the effort, she dragged herself the remaining distance and threw open the door.

"Gabby!" she screamed. "Gabby, come back!"

She saw Gabby look out at her, then back at Tyler. She opened the car door and got out, standing there a moment as if undecided. The lace of the dress moved. Robin was sure it rustled, talking to Gabby, whispering to Gabby, Go back. Go back. Get in the car.

"Be strong, Gabby," Robin whispered. "Come back. I love you, Gabby." Then familiar blackness closed in, and she fell.

She was in her own house when she awakened. Anxious faces bent over her. Her mother. Gabby. Tyler.

"Gabby," she whispered.

"I'm okay," Gabby said. She looked pale, but Robin was relieved to see that she wore her usual jeans and a long-sleeved shirt now.

Robin was too tired to ask what happened.

Gabby didn't wait for her to ask.

"There's something wrong with that dress," she said in a shaky voice. "It's almost as if it *asked* me to wear it. I couldn't resist looking at it when I took it home, and then it *wanted* me to wear it." Her voice broke.

Robin reached out to take her hand. "I know, Gabby. You don't have to talk about it."

But Gabby rubbed her sleeve across her nose like a little kid and went on. "Tyler and I saw you fall. We came running in. Miss Catherine was raving something about Michael and the prom dress. She came toward me as if she were going to do something to me."

Gabby put her hand over her face for a moment. "She scared me," she said. "I ran home and took the dress off. Tyler didn't want me wearing it in the first place."

"Bad vibes," Tyler said. "After your accident, I didn't like it anymore."

"She's not Miss Catherine," Robin whispered.

Tyler nodded. "The police are trying to untangle that whole story. They took Rowena away. She kept yelling that you stole the prom dress and her beau."

Robin said, "I only took the dress because I wanted to look beautiful for you."

He looked hurt and puzzled. "Do you believe I'm the kind of guy who cares more about a dress than the girl inside it?"

She smiled. "Thank you, Tyler. Would you do something for me? Would you take the dress up to the attic and hang it in Miss Catherine's, I mean, Rowena's little closet behind the chimney?" That was the best thing to do with it. Just bury it away up there now that Rowena had been taken away. Bury it where it would stay until the house rotted away and tumbled down around it. She could almost see the house crumbling, falling in on itself. Yes, let the house destroy the dress.

"I'll take it up there." Tyler sat down on the bed beside her and kissed her gently. "The doctor is coming to check you out soon. But you need some sleep now, Cinderella. Those casts aren't exactly glass slippers, but they'll make it so that one day we'll go to a ball again."

She smiled at him. She felt sure he was right. She'd walk again. Dance. Someday she'd be able to pick up her dream.

The old Macfarlane house was still vacant when Robin and her family moved to another town, where she could be closer to a rehabilitation hospital. And where Robin would be away from that house, so filled with awful memories. It wasn't so far away from Forest Dale that Tyler couldn't visit frequently. When the story of Catherine and Rowena hit the newspapers, he brought them for her to see.

After Rowena was taken to a psychiatric hospital, investigations turned up most of the facts. Reporters found elderly people who had known the twin sisters, and they interviewed them. They read old letters and even discovered Michael, the handsome "beau" both sisters had wanted. However Michael, still handsome despite his years, could contribute nothing; his memories were gone, wiped out by Alzheimer's disease. His children said he'd never mentioned either Catherine or Rowena.

Piece by piece, the reporters put together the story. They wrote of the acid incident all those years ago and how Rowena had been sent away to an asylum. Catherine moved somewhere far away from Forest Dale, where no one she knew would ever see her hideously scarred face.

Rowena had eventually been released into Catherine's custody. Here the story took an even uglier turn. The sisters had lived as recluses. No one ever saw them. Then one day there was a devastating fire. Rowena was burned to death, and Catherine came back to live in Forest Dale, in the old family home. At least, everyone thought it was Catherine because of the scar, until the day she retreated into the world of total insanity and admitted she was Rowena. And in her ravings she told of setting the fire that killed

Catherine, but only after the scar on her own face healed. She'd gouged out her birthmark to create a scar very much like the one the acid had made on Catherine's cheek, so she could take over her sister's identity, taking the house, and, in her fantasies, Michael.

Robin was relieved when Tyler told her that the old house was going to be torn down. She pictured the wrecking ball crashing into the old walls, collapsing the attic, burying the dress beneath tons of rubble, where it would never be seen again.

And that would be the end of it.

The owner of the antique shop, Attic Treasures, knew she'd truly found a treasure when she opened the almost-hidden attic door in the old house and discovered the dresses. There were three of them. Gleefully, she carried them off to her shop, congratulating herself on buying everything that was inside the old house before it was torn down.

She hung the dresses on the rack in her shop. Surely someone would want those dresses, especially the cream-colored lace one. A real beauty.

It was there at Attic Treasures that Natalie found just what she'd been looking for. She needed the perfect dress to try out for an important part in a play. She needed the perfect dress that would set her apart from all the other aspiring young actresses.

The lace dress was perfect. It rustled sweetly

when she touched it, speaking softly of the wonders that would come to her if she wore it. What a dress it was!

But the price was too high. Too much. She couldn't afford to pay a price like that.

She turned to the dress next to it, a red one with long, slithery fringes. Nice. A little less expensive.

But the lace dress called to her, begged her to look at it again.

She fingered its soft folds.

Putting down the shopping bag she'd gotten in another store, she took the lace dress from its hanger and held it up against her while she looked in the three-way mirror.

The dress lit up her honey-colored hair and gave her skin a soft glow. She'd never looked so good before — except for something dark on her left cheek. What was it? She brushed at it, and it disappeared. Just a shadow in the mirror. That was all.

She had to have this dress. Rob Walters was directing the coming play, and he'd already said he loved her low, throaty voice, the voice she was so proud of, the voice she worked on endlessly to make rich and strong. Rob would adore her in this dress. She'd be sure to get the part. And maybe even Rob.

Glancing around to make sure the proprietor of the shop was busy in the back, Natalie swiftly stuffed the dress into her shopping bag and hurried from the store.

Tomorrow she would wear the dress!

About the Author

LAEL LITTKE grew up in Mink Creek, Idaho, where she dreamed of becoming a writer while she rode her horse over the hills to fetch the cows. She went on to study writing at Utah State University, from which she holds a B.S. degree. After she married, she took writing classes wherever she lived — Denver, New York City, Washington, D.C., and Pasadena, California, where she now lives with her husband, George, seven cats, and two dogs, and her daughter, Lori, nearby. She has published approximately seventy-five short stories of all types and nine books for young people, including *Shanny on Her Own*, which was a Junior Literary Guild selection and was on the International Reading Association's Young Adult Choices list for 1987. She also teaches occasional classes in writing at Pasadena City College and UCLA.

point®

Other books you will enjoy,
about real kids like you!